the
mushroom man

 *the*
mushroom
man

sophie powell

G. P. PUTNAM'S SONS
NEW YORK

G. P. Putnam's Sons
Publishers Since 1838
a member of
Penguin Putnam Inc.
375 Hudson Street
New York, NY 10014

Library of Congress Cataloging-in-Publication Data

Powell, Sophie, date.
The mushroom man / Sophie Powell.
p. cm.
ISBN 0-399-14963-5
1. Mothers and daughters—Fiction. 2. Missing children—
Fiction. 3. Country life—Fiction. 4. Sisters—Fiction.
5. Widows—Fiction. 6. Wales—Fiction. I. Title.
PR6116.O95 M87   2003   2002021355
823'.92—dc21

Printed in the United States of America
1   3   5   7   9   10   8   6   4   2

This book is printed on acid-free paper. ∞

Book design by Stephanie Huntwork

For my mother

Thanks to Nicholas Christopher, my teacher, and my NYU Creative Writing colleagues, for their invaluable guidance and encouragement. Thanks to Aimee Taub, a fabulous editor, and Faye Bender, my agent, for placing their confidence in me. Thanks to Anna Jardine. And thanks to my family and friends for their love, support, and inspiration—especially my Polish grandmother, Josephine Lomnicka, for introducing me to mushrooms, and my Welsh grandmother, Lillian Powell, for introducing me to Celtic folklore, and my mother and father for magical holidays with my sister, Katie, and brother, David, on the Welsh hill farm that provides the setting for this story.

i

Every year Mrs. Griffiths writes, Dear Charlotte, please come and visit, and every year Mrs. Newman writes back, Next year, next year. Until Mrs. Griffiths picks up the telephone receiver one morning in August and dials an unfamiliar number. She tells Mrs. Newman she wants to see her. She tells Mrs. Newman she finds it upsetting. She tells Mrs. Newman she wants to see her six-year-old niece.

Come for a week at the end of the month, Charlotte. Just come on your own with Lily if Richard's too busy.

And Mrs. Newman can't think fast enough to say no.

Beth slowly slots the receiver back into place, takes a sip of chamomile tea, and wanders outside. Her eyes skim past her fields, past her tumulus, past her plum trees, past her stream, toward her forest, where her triplets have gone mushroom picking, where her son is making love to his girlfriend, and where two years ago she scattered her husband's ashes.

1

Charlotte sinks into the smothering smell of her leather-lined Jaguar, slams the door, and turns on the ignition to open her electric window and say a few last words to her husband.

Everything's on the piece of paper on the notice board: the address, Pavlova's cell-phone number in case you run into any problems on your own at home when she's not in —

I'll be fine.

I'm only a phone call away.

Don't worry about me. Just try and enjoy yourself.

Enjoy myself!

She's your sister, Charlotte.

She sniffs. He strokes her cheek and makes a funny face at his daughter in the backseat.

Pthththeewwwwwwww. Lily blows a raspberry at him, squidging her face against the window.

Charlotte shakes her head, reminds him about watering the geraniums, and drives off listening to Schubert on classical FM.

Mr. Newman watches his wife's car disappear around the corner, stretches his arms and hands out, and walks back inside the house to make a call to someone's cell phone.

It's her voice mail. He leaves a message.

It's me. She's gone. Come around as soon as you can.

He puts the telephone receiver down. He feels naughty. He fills a jug up with water and goes over to the geraniums to make himself feel better.

Beth is cooking, the triplets are cleaning, and Joseph and his girlfriend are supposed to be clearing up the yard. The house smells of soap and lamb cutlets and expectation, and the record player is spinning out Spanish dances.

Beth is chopping. Swollen tomatoes, waxy aubergines, fleshy mushrooms. Chop chop chop. Into triangles and rectangles and parallelograms. Chop chop chop. Skinned home-grown swedes, skinned home-grown onions, skinned home-grown carrots. Chop chop chop. Under the knife, into the pans, onto the hob.

Samantha, Jude, and Amy are sweeping the dead bluebottle flies off the windowsills and then washing the surfaces down with soapy water. They whirl and wiggle to the beat in between windows and wolf whistle at the end of each track. Jude says she'll learn to dance the flamenco when she visits Amy, who has married her bullfighter in Madrid and has a pink-grapefruit tree in her front garden. Sam says she'll bring them both back some shark meat when she's become a Filipino pirate. They each blow a bubble with the soapy water through their thumb and index finger curled into closed, crablike pincers, and make a wish that they'll all live to be one hundred: Mum and Sam and Jude and Amy and Joseph. Amen.

But Joseph already feels he is with the angels.

Joseph is under Nest, on the grass, out of sight. Joseph sees blueness and brilliance and golden halos and wants to stay like this forever. He plucks off a buttercup near his shoulder, slots it behind Nest's ear, and asks her to do it to him again.

⌐☾

When it comes down to it, Mrs. Newman is ashamed of her sister. Ashamed that she sunk herself to *him,* ashamed that she chose to live *his* way of life, ashamed that she continued to live *his* way of life when *he* died and deserted four directionless, unprovided-for children.

And Beth didn't upset only her. She upset their mother, who wasn't well anyway and didn't need this kind of worry, and she upset their father, who did a job he didn't like to send them to the best private schools, to make sure they went to the best universities, to make sure they had the best opportunities. Things were expected of them, things should be fulfilled by them, things should be paid back by them.

But not by Beth. Beth didn't even try. Beth just went and married a not-even-a-carpenter and went and lived in the middle of nowhere in Wales. A not-even-a-carpenter who didn't even make his own stuff, a not-even-a-carpenter who just repaired and tarted up old, worn furniture and tried to make it look spanking new.

Beth devastated all of them, and Charlotte could never forgive her. Not even when *he* died and Beth was left on her own with her mistakes. Not even when Beth sends the Christmas cards and birthday cards and Easter cards, which the children make with a gold-glitter border, and the long letters, which always invite her to come and stay. But Charlotte is coming to visit Beth because she has always had a sense of duty, because she wants to display her sense of duty, and because she thinks Beth's children could do with seeing someone with a sense of duty.

Mummy, can I have another pink marshmallow? asks Lily in the back, in the stuffy heat, in a traffic jam.

You've had enough, Mummy replies. You'll rot your teeth.

Pleeeeeeeeeeezz.

I said no.

Pavlova always lets me have as many sweets as I want.

And I say no.

℀

Pavlova is sitting in Kensington Gardens writing a letter to her bedridden mother in her bugridden bed-sit in Estonia. She has four banana skins on the lawn beside her, because she can't get enough of all the bananas in the shops in England, and she chews a piece of cola-flavored Hollywood gum to get a tang of golden America and all the priceless designer dresses at movie premieres.

She writes to her mother about the theaters, the cell phone she has been given, the coffee shops, and Charlotte's electric foot massager. She writes about everything apart from the main thing, the oops-I'm-fucking-my-employer-but-he-slips-me-extra-cash-and-buys-me-little-almond-biscuits-in-a-little-glittery-tin thing.

But the truth is, it's not the main thing for Pavlova, it's the mean-medium-mode if-I-didn't-do-it-everybody-would-be-surprised thing for Pavlova. Pavlova fucks her bosses all the time back home; it gets her power, it gets her glamour, it gets her money to buy tickets for flights to England to fuck other bosses.

She turns her phone back on, listens to her new voice message, and leaving the banana skins where they are for someone else to pick up, heads for more little almond biscuits.

⁀

When it comes down to it, Mrs. Griffiths is hurt by her sister's behavior. Hurt by the way she never replies to her letters. Hurt by the way she never sends the children birthday cards. Hurt by the way she only ever sends the same formal, leftover-looking Christmas card.

Of course, she knows what Charlotte thinks, she knows Charlotte's unyielding opinion: the opinion you can smell in the definite dot she always adds at the end of her signature on her Christmas cards. Beth knows, but she doesn't understand it. Beth knows, but she can't understand why Charlotte doesn't just accept it. Like Mum accepts it, and has even begun to understand it. Like Dad accepts it, and tries to understand it.

But Charlotte doesn't even try. Charlotte told her she was throwing her life away, and ever since Lily was born, they don't even nibble on burnt mince pies together anymore, on Boxing Day, at their parents' house.

And Charlotte upsets everyone. She upsets her mother and her father, who would love to have them all together with the kids playing Monopoly, and the burnt mince pies, and she upsets the triplets, who not once in their eleven years have received a birthday card from their godmother.

☙

Now Lily, we're nearly there and I have a few things I want you to remember. Charlotte glances in the rearview mirror at her daughter, who is sticking her finger right up her nostril and wiggling it all around.

Lily!

I'll remember better if I have a pink marshmallow.

You'll remember better indeed if you have a hard slap on the wrist.

Lily puts her hands between her legs and peers up at her mother's odd-looking headrest, framed by a mass of sculptured, highlighted curls.

We're going to a very different place, Lily, with very different people, people who live very differently to us. Do you understand what I mean, Lily?

Like the giant in "Jack and the Beanstalk"?

Not quite like the giant, darling. Let me start from the beginning. These children live on a farm and don't have a daddy like you do—

Like Jack. Jack didn't have a daddy and lived on a farm.

Well, yes, I suppose a bit like Jack, although they certainly don't have any golden-egg-laying hens, that's for sure. She sniffs. To put it frankly, Lily, they're rather wild and I don't want you to catch anything nasty. I don't want you to share their towels—I want you to remember to use the ones Mummy has packed for you—and I don't want you to share any of their cups or plates or cutlery before you've made sure they've been thoroughly washed beforehand. Do you understand, darling?

Do they have normal hens?

Never mind the hens, I've no idea whether they've got any hens. But do you understand what I said about hygiene, Lily, about the towels and cups and plates and cutlery?

Lily sticks her finger up her nostril again.

~❧~

Beth hurries down to the bottom of the garden to dump her vegetable skins, and waves back at Jude calling out to her from the open bathroom window.

Will they be here soon?

Any minute. Are you changed?

Changed?

I ironed you each a clean pair of shorts and T-shirt and hung them behind your door.

Jude quickly closes the window.

Excited voices, the patter of naked feet, bangs, laughter.

The color of sunlight about to disappear over to the other side of the world.

2

Hens! They've got hens! Lily explodes out of the car, runs at a right angle to the house toward the whitewashed stone hut, which was originally an outdoor toilet, and crouches down to spy on the shitting, clucking creatures she has frightened into the darkness.

Beth stands leaning her elbow on the open front gate, her face a detailed map of unfathomable laughing lines. The triplets, dressed in crisp clothes still smelling of lemon washing powder, are hovering with awkward arms behind her.

Charlotte takes a deep breath and slowly slides out the ignition key. She opens the door. Right foot on the ground. Left foot on the ground. And up, but not looking upward. She turns her back, steps to the left, and slams the door hard. She opens the trunk, takes out a large suitcase and a plastic bag containing Wellington boots, and slams the trunk closed.

She shuffles around to look at Beth.

Beth has put on weight. All Charlotte can see is the flab below her upper arm wobbling as she waves over to her.

⟨᠔⟩

You look well, Beth, says Charlotte. She stands stiff as she is en-snaked in Beth's flab and feels fat, wet lips on her cheek. She stares across at the triplets. Black-haired, like *him.* All in a row, identical, holding hands. Like cut-out paper dolls. As if she'd been hit on the head and had gone cross-eyed.

You remember the triplets.

Of course.

Sam and Jude and Amy.

Hi. At the same time. In the same tone. With the same smile.

And that must be Lily. Beth looks over at Lily still crouching out-side the hut, staring into the darkness and searching for golden eggs. She looks like an angel, Charlotte.

Lily! Lily turns her head. Come and say hello.

Lily reluctantly leaves her hens and walks toward the very differ-ent people who don't have a daddy.

Hello, my name's Lily. Do you have a beanstalk by any chance?

⟨᠔⟩

They're all touching Lily and they all have dirt under their finger-nails. Charlotte has seen the nails of only one of them, but she knows the same goes for all of them, the ½-of-*him* them, the 3X-*him* them. And now they even want to take her daughter away.

Just to the tumulus, one of them threatens. Just to the edge of the forest.

I'd rather Lily stayed with me.

Let her go, Lottie, conspires Beth. Let her stretch her legs after the long journey.

Please, Mummy. Please.

Well, be careful. And put your Wellies on. She hands Lily her red Wellies.

Lily sits on the doorstep, slips off her shoes, slips into her Wellies, places her shoes neatly together in the corner.

Don't worry, Auntie Charlotte. We'll look after her. It's the one she saw with the dirty nails.

Auntie Charlotte. Auntie Charlotte. Aun tee. Tee hee. Tee hee. Aun tee. The words multiply in her mind like bacteria.

They open a gate and disappear among overgrown grass and giant thistles.

❧

Pavlova opens the front door into the dark coolness of the hall.

Hallo.

She closes the door, dumps down her rucksack, and kicks off her sandals.

Hallo. Louder.

I'm in the drawing room.

She walks with sticky bare feet down the corridor into the drawing room. Mr. Newman is sprawled out on the sofa, reading Homer's *Odyssey* in the original, a glass of sherry on the Chinese rug below him.

He puts his book down and pats the sofa.

She smiles, takes his head in her hands, and thrusts her warm tongue down his throat.

Beth hands Charlotte a glass of freshly squeezed orange juice with three cubes of ice.

Thanks.

Pleasure.

Beth hears Charlotte's ice making a popping sound and just wants to run up and hug her again. Her little grown-up sister. Her little grown-apart sister. She even has a different Charlotte smell now.

It's so good to have you and Lily to stay.

Charlotte pretends to be preoccupied with sipping her orange juice.

Beth turns her back to check the vegetables unnecessarily.

You'll love the farm, Charlotte. I'll take you for a quick tour tonight after dinner if it's not too dark. And you've come at just the right time of the year. It was so nice today all six of us had a dip in the stream.

All six of you?

Didn't I mention our new addition?

Charlotte looks blank.

Joseph's girlfriend, Nest?

Nest? Charlotte nearly chokes on an ice cube. A name? As in birds?

They're inseparable, like Siamese twins. She's the neighboring farmer's daughter, so she comes over all the time.

An agricultural name, reflects Charlotte. Of course it could only be an agricultural name.

She's a good girl. Doesn't say much, but she's got a lovely open face.

Bet she's got lovely open legs too, by the sound of it, Charlotte concludes.

And it's so nice for Joseph to have her company. I always worry that he feels left out, with the girls being so close and everything, and of course I don't really count.

Beth leans out the window. They shouldn't be far off from the house, actually. The triplets and Lily will probably bump into them.

⌀

They're naked! Lily charges down the slope in hysterics. There are two people in the field who are all naked!

Nest has done it to Joseph again. She slithers off and lies on her back, trying to catch the last few toe-tinglings. Joseph rolls the slimy thing off, contains the leftover white magic stuff in a knot, and puts it neatly in the corner next to the other one.

They lie side by side waiting for their sweat to dry in the evening coolness.

Willy! Boobies! Vagina! Lily cannot believe her luck.

Joseph and Nest turn around, see Lily, exchange looks, and yank on their clothes. Joseph covers the slimy things with earth.

⟨✦⟩

Charlotte follows Beth out of the kitchen, through the corridor past the living room and Beth's studio, up the stairs and down another corridor—past a bathroom, two bedrooms, an airing cupboard, and a stepladder leading up to the attic—until they reach the bedroom she and Lily will share. A spacious room, which has a large bay window overlooking the forest, with no curtains.

Here you go. I hope this is all right.

There are no curtains, Charlotte registers. There are no curtains!

I hope you don't mind there not being any curtains, I've just never seen the need, really.

We'll just have to get changed under the bedclothes, decides Charlotte. It's fine, she says.

Come downstairs as soon as you're unpacked.

Charlotte watches Beth drift out of the lopsided door frame and then turns to examine the curtainless room where she and Lily will be sleeping. A large double bed with a bluebell-flower-print sheet and a bedside table on either side. A solid wardrobe with a full-length mirror. A cream-painted chest of drawers that has on top of it a vase full of freshly picked lily of the valley and a framed photo of the children dressed up for Halloween and holding a glowing pumpkin with a zigzag mouth. On the papered walls are bookshelves, paintings, and two black candleholders above the bedposts.

This is the master bedroom, concludes Charlotte. This is where *he* slept and rubbed up snug and smug against my brainwashed sister.

She looks closer at the paintings: Trees. All trees. It was definitely *his* bedroom. All paintings of different types and angles and seasons of trees. There is even a framed chart of the Celtic Tree Calendar.

And the books? Charlotte runs her eye across the multicolored keyboard of book spines. Definitely Beth's. They're all poetry collections and romance novels.

Charlotte leans her hand on the windowsill, which is still damp from the triplets' washing, and pushes open the windows toward the thousands of different shades of green and orange-yellow that have seeped into the hills, and Lily's faint, invisible laughter.

⊸◯

Lily reminds Amy of an electric baby doll they once had, called Jemima. She needed two cylindrical batteries up her bottom and she was made with a permanent grin. Even when she fell flat on her face while she was crawling, even when you could get her to cry and wet her knickers by filling her up with water, even when their dog (who was run over a few months ago) chewed both her legs off, the same invincible grin beamed straight back at you.

Amy can't help treating Lily like a baby doll too. She touches her all the time, she wants to dress her in exotic flamenco dresses and braid her hair, she wants to take her to bed with her.

And she wants Lily to like her the best out of everyone.

She doesn't like it when Sam and Jude start giving Lily the bumps and Lily laughs and shouts, Again! Again! She doesn't like it when Nest lifts her up onto Joseph's shoulders and Lily laughs and shouts, Giddyup horsey, giddyup horsey!

So on the way up the slope back to the house, when they start to discuss taking Lily mushroom picking—Has she been mushroom picking before? Would she like to come? What about first thing to-morrow morning?—Amy starts to think of a mushroom fairy tale of her own to tell Lily as a bedtime story.

◦

When the children walk through the door, Beth is about to serve dinner and Charlotte is still upstairs, carefully hanging up her clothes and arranging her collection of cosmetics in neat rows on top of the chest of drawers.

Good walk? Beth asks, wafting away the hot vapor that erupts from the stove as she opens the top door.

Super, enthuses Lily, imitating her father in a cheerful mood. And we're going mushroom picking first thing tomorrow morning.

Oh, good. The triplets came back with a wonderful assortment of mushrooms a couple of days ago.

Where's Auntie Charlotte? asks Joseph.

Upstairs, unpacking. Could you fetch her, we're about to have dinner.

Joseph slips out of the kitchen.

The triplets and Nest go to the kitchen sink to wash their hands, and Amy draws up a chair for Lily and lifts her onto it so she can reach the tap.

Joseph knocks on Charlotte's door.

Charlotte opens it and jumps. He has grown to look exactly like *him*.

Hi, Auntie Charlotte. He is about to kiss her and then sees her expression. Dinner's ready.

⁂

Throughout the dinner, Charlotte cannot take her eyes off Nest's nipples. They protrude forth from her "Don't Look at Them" T-shirt like irresistible doorbell buttons. She wonders if you have to press one of them to get this Nest to speak. Because this Nest doesn't say anything, she even avoids saying thank you. She just watches and listens and smiles.

Beth doesn't feel awkward being with Charlotte because of the children sandwiched between them, and all of the food that has to be eaten. Beth doesn't hear the ice popping in Charlotte's water, because the children are talking so much and she's too busy answering questions. Lily is asking all about mushrooms: Which are the best ones, which are the poisonous ones, whether you die if you eat a poisonous one, whether you immediately die if you eat a definitely deadly one.

Toward the end, Lily turns to her mother. I can't wait to go mushroom picking tomorrow morning, Mummy.

Charlotte lets it go because she knows it's useless saying anything against it with the others there. She knows it's better to wait until she and Lily are alone in their room together—the door closed, the prospect of going home early and never coming back.

For dessert they eat homemade blueberry-and-apple pie. Joseph and Nest picked the blueberries that morning among the heather on the moor and Sam climbed the apple tree yesterday evening. The warm puff pastry melts on everybody's tongue, and the sugary fruit tastes of almost autumnal sunshine.

Outside, night is falling quickly and it begins to drizzle. The windows become mirrors, which Lily can't help pulling faces in, and everyone's cheeks are flushed with the heat from the stove.

Amy turns to Lily and asks if she would like to hear a fairy tale about the Mushroom Man as a bedtime story.

Lily knocks on the triplets' door when she has changed into her Peter Pan nightdress and brushed her teeth.

Come in.

All three are lying on their beds watching a gangster film on the television.

I've come for a bedtime story, announces Lily.

Yes, of course, Amy says. She switches off the television with the remote control.

Sam and Jude groan.

Come and sit on my bed. Amy pats the blanket. Lily closes the door and crawls up beside her. Amy puts her arm around Lily.

Once upon a time there was an old hermit with special fairy-seeing powers who lived alone in a wigwam in the forest. This Mushroom Man, as he was later to be called, saw how the fairies suffered in the rain—especially the Welsh fairies, because it rains all the time in Wales—and he was filled with pity for them: If the fairies were nowhere near shelter, they would get their pretty lace tutus and leaf ballet shoes all wet and dirty as the earth turned to muddy mush, and they would catch a fairy cough. One day the Mushroom Man couldn't stand it any longer. Wiping a tear from his eye, he said to himself, "Blow me if I don't help these poor little fairy creatures out!" So he set out for a rare visit to the village, to the library, to try to find out what he might do. But he didn't even need to get to the library to come up with the answer. He only had to get as far as the sweetshop on the corner, where the woman at the counter had a set of false teeth that fell out whenever she talked too much. It started to rain. He stood under the stripy sweetshop canopy and watched an old lady walk past.

"By Jove, I've got it!" he exclaimed. "How silly of me not to have thought of it before! Umbrellas is what Mankind has, and umbrellas is what the fairy creatures shall have too!"

So the Mushroom Man skipped all the way back home in excitement and immediately set to making mini-umbrellas of all colors, shapes, and sizes, to fit and suit the fairy race: button mushrooms for baby fairies, short mushrooms with wide tops for dumpy fairies, white-spotted red ones for fashion-conscious fairies . . .

And whenever there was a rainy patch, he would plant the fairy umbrellas together in groups in the ground at night. In groups because fairies are sociable creatures and don't usually wander around alone. At night because, as a hermit, the Mushroom Man wanted to avoid bumping into Mankind.

As you can imagine, the fairies were over the moon. "Oh, look!" They squeaked. "No more dirtying our pretty lace tutus and leaf ballet shoes! No more fairy coughs!" They called their umbrellas "mushrooms," rooms safe from the muddy mush, and they honored their Mushroom Man, as they called him, with a wish.

"Your wish," proclaimed Princess Fairymostbeautiful to the Mushroom Man after the first appearance of the mushrooms, handing him a leaf cup of fairy plum juice, "is our command."

The Mushroom Man took a thoughtful sip of fairy plum juice, and, kneeling at the leaf ballet shoes of Princess Fairymostbeautiful and gazing up at the diamond pupils of her eyes and the golden lipstick on her lips, he addressed the golden-haired Lady of the Forest.

"Princess Fairymostbeautiful, diamond-eyed, golden-lipped Lady of the Forest, I wish that I may become a fairy like you—residing, immortal and invisible, in one of your sumptuous tree palaces and drinking fairy plum juice out of leaf cups all day whilst making your mushroom umbrellas."

Princess Fairymostbeautiful nodded and sprinkled him with golden fairy dust. "You shall reside in the most sumptuous tree palace after mine, o inventive Mushroom Man." There was a bellowing burst of thunder and a zigzag flare of lightning, and the Mushroom Man grew smaller and smaller and more and more transparent until he dissolved into the fresh forest air like a boiled sweet on the tongue.

And so the Mushroom Man lives happily ever after, immortal and invisible, in a sumptuous tree palace with hundreds of red-velvet-curtained chambers with emerald chandeliers, drinking fairy plum juice out of leaf cups all day whilst making the fairies their mushroom umbrellas.

Amy slows down and quiets to a whisper with her last sentence.

Sam and Jude exchange looks and smile. There is a moment of silence, as if they're all waiting for the ɟ at the end of Amy's final word to flutter up and away into the air and catch up with its flock of friends.

Where are the fairy palaces in the trees? asks Lily.

All around, Amy answers. Around each tree is an invisible fairy palace. The trunk and branches and twigs and leaf veins are the motorway, the dual-carriage ways, the normal roads, and the foot-paths to the different parts of the palace, respectively.

And what do they travel in? inquires Lily. Carriages?

Exactly, Amy replies. Unicorn-driven carriages which leave their tiny thin tracks on the bark, as you can see.

There's a knock on the door. The light from the corridor floods in.

Come on, Lily. It's past your bedtime.

Lily's face falls. She turns to Amy. What time are we going mush-room picking tomorrow morning?

As soon as you're up, before breakfast.

I'm up at seven.

We'll go at quarter past seven, then.

☙

You're not going mushroom picking tomorrow morning, says her mother—when they're alone together, the door closed.

Lily bursts into tears. Please, Mummy. Please.

Absolutely not.

Pavlova would let me.

Pavlova's a lazy slut, snaps Charlotte, surprised at herself.

☙

Mr. Newman watches Pavlova's naked torso disappear through the doorway to go downstairs for a glass of water.

He picks up the telephone receiver to call Charlotte's cell phone.

It's her voice mail. He leaves a message.

It's me. Just ringing to make sure you're okay. I'll call you again tomorrow.

He puts the phone down. He can still taste Pavlova's warm, juicy fullness. He goes to brush his teeth.

3

Lily is awoken by a thick finger of sunlight spilling in through the window and forming a warm pool over her face and pillow. She glances at the clock on the bedside table: six thirty-three, the hands one smooth black line pointing downward.

She turns slowly to check on her mother. She is sleeping—face upward, curlers in her hair, a thin stream of dribble streaking her chin. Lily examines the small mole on her neck before slipping out of bed and out the door, as silently as an exhaled breath.

She tiptoes to the bathroom to pee. She sits on the toilet thinking about the Mushroom Man until she supposes it is seven o'clock and she can wake the others.

Lily knocks on the triplets' door. Silence. She knocks again.

Come in.

They are all still in bed. The room smells of slept-in stuffiness.

I'm ready to go mushroom picking.

Amy sits up and looks at Lily in her nightdress, hovering in the doorway—straight back, tiny bare feet together, tiny hands folded into a ball in front of her. A cross between a soldier and a ballerina.

Jude and Sam remain motionless.

Sure. Amy shakes Sam in the bed next to her. Let's all get changed.

Lily wrinkles up her forehead. She's completely forgotten about getting changed. But she knows that if she goes back into the bedroom her mother will hear her and stop her from going.

Can I borrow some of your clothes?

I think they'll be a little big for you. Don't you want to wear your own? Amy watches Lily rub her thumbs around and around each other.

If I go back into my room Mummy will hear me and stop me going. In one long breath.

Stop her going? Amy wonders. She gets out of bed and takes Lily's soft hand.

Come with me, she says. I'm sure we can find something in the airing cupboard.

Lily follows her out of the room. In the airing cupboard Amy finds Joseph's old Ninja Turtles shorts, a small pair of odd socks, the Kellogg's Coco Pops T-shirt Jude sent away for when she had collected enough tokens, and the yellow sweater Amy's Welsh grandmother knitted for her as a birthday present when she was younger.

And some panties, whispers Lily. I'm not wearing any panties.

They walk down the front field toward the forest. The dewy grass washes their Wellingtons, and the still air is chill and drowsy. Joseph and Sam are holding the baskets, knives, and flashlights. Nest is scouring the hedgerow for ripe hazelnuts.

It's going to be a good morning for mushrooms, augurs Sam.

They all nod in agreement and look toward the forest overflowing into the horizon for confirmation.

Lily has run ahead. She paddles in the stream at the edge of the forest and feels the current against her red Wellingtons. She wonders whether it is bad to pick the mushrooms if they are meant for the fairies, she wonders whether the fairies and the Mushroom Man become angry.

In the forest, everyone is quiet, and Joseph and Nest wander off together without anyone else's acknowledging it.

Lily wants to ask questions, but she feels she can't. Lily wants to tell them not to pick any mushrooms, but she feels she would be breaking a rule. So she just follows the others, stares at the damp, dark ground, listens to their footsteps and the faraway screeching of a buzzard, smells earth and pine and rotting leaves. Hoping they don't find any fairy umbrellas to take away from the fairies.

But families of fairy umbrellas are soon spotted across the forest floor, thrusting their faces up from it like archipelagos of exotic islands. Multicolored, slimy, spongy fungi.

Midnight-blue boletes! Sam takes one knife from her basket and hands the other to Amy, who is standing nearest her. They both stoop, pinch the stalk of a big bolete with their left thumb and index finger, slice through with the knife in their right hand, and carefully place the mushroom upside down in the basket. They keep doing this. Pinch, slice, place upside down. Pinch, slice, place upside down. Pinch, slice, place upside down. Pinch, slice, place upside down.

Amy looks up at Lily wincing—eyes shut, hands clenched. Are you all right, Lily? Lily opens her eyes. Do you want a go?

Lily shakes her head. It isn't right. She looks as if she's about to cry. I'm going back to the house.

She turns and runs.

Amy drops her knife, goes after her, grabs her delicate shoulders, turns her around.

What's wrong, Lily? Don't you like the mushroom picking?

No. She tries to shake herself free.

I'll take you back to the house.

I want to go on my own.

Amy reluctantly lets her go and watches her run off toward the light at the edge of the forest.

She walks back to Sam and Jude.

❧

Beth is awoken by a persistent bluebottle fly buzzing and butting at the window. She gets up from the mattress in the attic, where she has been sleeping, opens the window, and watches the bluebottle bump toward the gap until it zooms off out into soothing cotton clouds.

She puts on her dressing gown and slippers, climbs down the stepladder, glances at Charlotte's blank, closed door, and enters the bathroom. She shuts the door, pushes the bath plug down, turns on the bathwater, and adds half a cup of strawberry sundae bubble bath, her favorite.

She undresses and contemplates the top half of herself in the mirror above the sink. All she sees is saggy breasts and droopy nipples. All she sees is the texture of flesh becoming accustomed to loneliness.

She turns off the taps and steps into her warm bath.

❧

I'm surprised she's not weirder, with a mother like that, Jude says.

Bored with the midnight-blue boletes, they have moved on to a crop of Saint George's. Pinch, slice, place upside down. Pinch, slice, place upside down.

She's not weird, Amy corrects. She's just little. Little kids go funny all the time.

But I thought she wanted to go mushroom picking, persists Jude.

Sam places the last Saint George's mushroom in the basket and stands up. I think we've got enough, she says.

They start to head back.

Auntie Charlotte's going to be angry, says Amy.

We've done nothing wrong, answers Sam.

I should have gone with her, says Amy.

She's fine, answers Sam.

But what if something happens to her? says Amy.

Like what? answers Sam.

They climb over the fence at the end of the forest and jump over the stream into the field.

⊸ℓ◯

Joseph misses his dad. Joseph misses having another male presence around the farm so that the burden doesn't rest entirely on him. It's no use for Nest to tell him that there isn't a burden: Burden? What burden? What you talking about? It's no use pretending to himself that it's all right because Dad's around anyway, only in spirit form (as his mum always rambles on about): even if you swallow that baloney, what bloody good is a spirit going to do except scare the shit out of everyone? Joseph can feel the burden in the spare chair at the end of the table. Joseph can taste the burden in the extra effort his mum makes with the cooking. Joseph can see the burden in the way his mum eats and eats and eats and has done only two paintings in the past year—both still lifes, both of bowls of going-off fruit in front of half-opened windows. The burden is stuck with him like a puppy

34

he has been given for Christmas that can't be potty-trained: he knows he can't keep on living with it, but he doesn't have the heart to put it down.

Nest says, I'm going to give you a big fat love bite on your neck so your auntie Charlotte will have something else to be grossed out by.

Not now, Joseph answers. Just tell me you want me.

⌒⌒

Charlotte rolls to her side and sees the empty space next to her. There is only the ruffled imprint of Lily's small head on the pillow.

She waits and listens.

She gets up and checks inside the wardrobe and the chest of drawers to see if all Lily's clothes are still there. She pulls on her dressing gown and walks down the corridor.

Through the open doors of the bedrooms she can see that all the beds are empty.

There is no sound coming from downstairs.

She stops at the closed bathroom door. She can hear a tap dripping. Lily? No answer.

She knocks. Lily? It's me, Mummy.

She can hear sudden, heavy movement in bathwater.

Sorry, Beth. Charlotte addresses the closed door as if she can see through it. Have you seen Lily?

I've only just got up. Beth's voice is distant, an echo. She's probably gone mushroom picking. Weren't they all planning to go mushroom picking first thing this morning?

the mushroom man

When the triplets crash into the kitchen with their basketful of mushrooms, Beth is frying bacon and eggs and slices of fresh tomatoes and Charlotte is sitting straight-backed at the table with her eyes fixed out the window. Her black coffee is untouched in front of her, and her fingertips with their long, perfect nails are pressed down on the edge of the table as if she were about to start playing a piano.

We've picked tons, says Sam.

They were everywhere, says Jude.

Leave them on the table for now, says Beth.

Sam places the basket on the table. There is a sharp stench, like damp moss.

Charlotte thinks of witches coming back with ingredients for their potions.

Is Lily with Joseph and Nest? asks Charlotte.

Amy feels a whoosh at the pit of her stomach.

She wanted to come home on her own, Amy mumbles. She should be back any minute. I thought she'd already be back.

Charlotte panics. Where did you leave her? she demands, as the worst scenarios fast-forward in her imagination.

At the edge of the forest, answers Amy.

The forest! Charlotte stands. Did you see her leave the forest?

Not exactly.

When did you last see her?

Amy looks at Sam. Sam looks at the clock with the sunshine face on the kitchen wall. The sound of spitting fat from the frying pan.

About three quarters of an hour ago, answers Sam.

I'm off to find her, announces Charlotte, seething, as she makes for the door.

Beth grips her arm.

Calm down, Charlotte, says Beth. Stay here. The girls will go. You wouldn't know where to look. She turns to the triplets. Go and find her, she orders — voice firm but eyes sympathetic. All of you. Right away. You shouldn't have left her like that.

They file out of the kitchen in silence.

Beth turns the radio on, brings the mushroom basket over to the counter, fishes out a midnight-blue bolete, and starts chopping.

Mr. Newman likes Pavlova in the morning best of all. He likes the way her long blond hair is knotty and disordered. He likes the way her cheeks are flushed a delicate pink. He likes the way she is already naked and he can just open her fat legs and stick it right in. And her moaning! God, her moaning turns him on. It's the softest moaning, but it makes him go all hard and hot and worked up. She sometimes whispers things in Estonian too, and then he wants to furrow into her wetness so deep that she tries to push him off, she's in so much pleasure.

But he's still waiting to get kinky with her. He's still waiting for the moment when he sees her full figure all zipped up in tight black leather like Catwoman in *Batman* and she whips him and bites him until he bleeds. He knows he really will be in seventh heaven then. He knows he really won't be able to get anything better than that.

Mr. Newman opens her legs and starts rubbing himself on her belly to work himself up.

Pavlova likes Mr. Newman in the morning least of all. She dislikes the way she's not woozy enough with wine anymore to overlook the fact that she's fucking a fifty-year-old with bad teeth and a you-know-what that goes floppy after less than two minutes. She dislikes the way that her wake-up call is to feel his dirty rubbing on her belly. At times like these, she wonders what she's doing. At times like these, she doesn't think about the cash, or the little almond biscuits, or the getting-a-kick-out-of-the-not-supposed-to-ness of it all. She just feels sluttish and foolish and lonely. She just wants to go home and have an ordinary job and an ordinary husband and an ordinary life like her sister.

But she knows that as soon as she gets home she will change her mind.

She closes her eyes and starts to moan to pretend she's enjoying herself.

⁓〇

They see Lily crossing the stream and run down the slope to meet her. She looks happy: her naked knees are speckled with mud, her chubby cheeks are like rosy apples, her eyes are lively and laughing.

You're wrong about not being able to see the Mushroom Man, she tells Amy. You're wrong that he's invisible to Mankind like the fairies. The Mushroom Man just now came up to me when I was walking in the forest on my own and gave me a piece of Turkish delight like the White Witch gave Edmund in *The Lion, the Witch and the Wardrobe*. He asked me what my name was and where I lived, and when I asked him wasn't it bad to pick the mushrooms if they were meant for the fairies, he said no, it's absolutely fine, he likes giving pleasure to Mankind as well as to the fairies.

Is that where you've been then, in the forest? asks Amy. I thought you were going back to the house.

I *was* going back to the house, but then I bumped into the Mushroom Man and stopped to have a chat. He's got a beard like Father Christmas, by the way, and he's got a fat belly from drinking too much fairy plum juice.

Amy and Jude each take one of Lily's hands and swing her up the slope toward the house.

When Charlotte sees her daughter entering the kitchen in clothes that aren't her own and with muddy knees, she immediately hauls her upstairs for a bath and a scolding and a hard slap on the wrist, even though Beth has already started to serve breakfast.

4

That afternoon, Charlotte drives down to the village because Beth has run out of milk. She wanted to take Lily with her, but Lily is getting all sticky and excited making rhubarb turnover cake with Beth. But Charlotte's glad to be away from the house, glad to be away from the constant, heavy cooking, glad to be away from Beth's constant, inconsequential, chirpy chitchat. And she's particularly glad to be away from the triplets, who make her feel dizzy and give her the creeps—those natal anomalies who have all got the same nervous twitch in their left cheek, and *his* dark, bushy eyebrows, which cling to the pale skin above their eyes like fat black leeches.

Oh God!

Splat in the middle of the road in front of her stands a loose sheep, staring stupidly straight at her.

She toots the horn.

Budge! She toots the horn again. Budge, lamb chops!

But the sheep just lets out a long stream of hot piss.

Her cell phone starts to ring.

Hello?

I've got through!

Richard, this isn't a good time. I'm stuck behind a sheep!

Behind a sheep?

I'm in the middle of bloody nowhere stuck behind a sheep!

Calm down.

I'm having a terrible time, but this has to take the biscuit. . . .

I tried to call you last night.

They left Lily alone in a forest, and there's not one single curtain in the whole house.

And Beth and the children? Are they all well?

Richard, this really isn't a good time. Charlotte switches off her phone and roars the engine.

The sheep starts to gallop for its life now, but still sticks to the middle of the road. Charlotte has an intimate view of the bopping, shitty bottom, right up to the outskirts of the village, where the sheep is suddenly inspired to dart off to the side and collapse with exhaustion.

⌒

After Beth has let Lily lick the cake batter from the sides of the mixing bowl, Amy asks her cousin if she wants to play hide-and-seek by the tumulus.

Sam and Jude are down there already, Amy says. Wanna come?

Yes, please. Lily grins with a cake-batter moustache.

Beth unties Lily's apron, which comes down to her feet like Cinderella's ball gown, and gives her a paper towel with a leaf print to wipe her mouth and hands.

Lily jumps down from the chair she has been standing on and follows Amy out of the kitchen to the porch to put on her red Wellingtons.

Stick together this time, Beth shouts after them.

⚭

Mr. Newman is sitting in a deck chair under the willow tree in the garden, with a beaker of mango juice and a custard cream doughnut, and he can pinpoint when it all started to go wrong: 10:33 P.M. on 22 July 1996, when Lily first poked her head out into the world. From that minute, Charlotte suddenly lost interest in him. From that minute, Charlotte suddenly stopped asking him about how his day had been when he came home from work; Charlotte suddenly stopped making him his favorite boeuf bourguignonne with potatoes dauphinoise on a Monday night; Charlotte suddenly stopped composing the little piano ditties that she would perform for him every Saturday afternoon after they had spent a lazy morning in bed together drinking freshly ground Jamaica Blue Mountain coffee and reading each other snippets out of the papers. It all became Lily. All Charlotte ever thought about or talked to him about was Lily.

At first, he understood it: he was as familiar with the distinct disinfectant smell of the IVF clinic as he was with his favorite chesterfield sofa in the Oxford and Cambridge Club, and he knew how long it had taken until they finally had their own child. He also expected it not to last. But it did—it does—and that's the problem. That's why he feels neglected, that's why he's reading his classics texts from university, that's why he's fucking Pavlova. For a bit of comfort: like a good pint in his club at the end of a hard day's work, like a warm hot-cross bun for elevenses.

He finishes off his custard doughnut, licks his sticky fingers, and goes back to Circe and her half-human pigs.

Sam and Jude are sitting cross-legged opposite each other on a rug at the top of the tumulus. They are testing each other on bone names for their biology exam at the beginning of the school term and they keep touching themselves as they point out which bones they are naming; it looks as if some bizarre religious ritual is being acted out. Come and play hide-and-seek, Amy calls up to them when she gets to the foot of the tumulus.

They both pull faces. We're learning the bones.

I told Lily we'd all play hide-and-seek. . . .

Lily waves to them, her fair hair glistening in the afternoon sunlight. Sam and Jude put their books aside and roll down the tumulus on their bellies.

I'll be seeker, declares Jude. She crouches, covers her eyes with her hands, her head bent down, and starts counting out loud. One, two, three . . .

The others scatter. Amy follows Lily, who heads for the forest.

◦◦◦

If there's one thing Charlotte can't resist, it's lace. Lace: she discovered it four years ago on an Easter holiday in Venice, and it reminds her of Victorian times and ladies in lovely long dresses with lovely long gloves and lovely pink parasols. She subscribes to *Lace Magazine* and was even enrolled in a bobbin-lace-making course, until she discovered all her classmates were industrial seamstresses. So when she spies the Little Welsh Bobbin Lace Shop on the corner, with a mannequin dressed in a lace bridal gown in the front window, she immediately crosses the road and opens the light-blue-painted door that goes ting-a-ling as she enters.

It's a feast of lace. She can't believe her luck. She is so captivated that she doesn't notice the fat old lady sitting behind a table who looks up from her crossword.

May I help you?

Charlotte jumps. The fat lady's cheeks are a web of thread-veins.

Just looking, thank you.

The bridal wear is at the back.

Charlotte nods. She runs her fingers over the piles of lace tablecloths, bedspreads, pillowcases, and even—she doesn't realize until she picks a pair up and looks closer—thongs.

They're comfortable too, you know, the fat lady says. I'm wearing one now, and it doesn't cut up or itch or anything.

Charlotte feels herself blushing, but her index finger can't stop tracing the beautifully tatted chain of daisy flowers.

I'll give the pair to you for twenty. They're usually twenty-five but I can see you like them a lot.

Charlotte finds herself handing the thong over and reaching in her purse. The fat lady wraps the thong up in lilac tissue paper and seals the packet with a circular sticker that says "With Best Wishes from the Little Welsh Bobbin Lace Shop." Charlotte stuffs the packet in her purse and hurries out the door into the sunlight, forgetting to say thank you.

She crosses the road and hurries toward the grocery.

$\bigcirc\hspace{-0.5em}\sim$

Amy crouches in a dried-up streambed in the forest. She has lost track of Lily, who went haring straight down an avenue of pines into the forest. Amy watches a legion of black ants carrying a dead daddy-longlegs, smells the doggy smell of foxes, and thinks about having to go back to school: she thinks about standing in a corner of the playground with her two sisters—giving everyone new nicknames and trying not to look at Felipe Llewellyn, who speaks fluent Spanish because his mother's Argentinean. She thinks about getting the part of Hermione in the Christmas play *The Winter's Tale*, about standing under the spotlight onstage in a long dress with lots of makeup and the clip-on amber earrings she has seen in the drama accessory box, about Felipe Llewellyn staring directly at her from the dark blur of the audience. She thinks about getting married to Felipe Llewellyn, who has taken up bullfighting in Madrid, with yellow rose petals being thrown all over her, about their whitewashed house with a pink-grapefruit tree in the front garden. She thinks about their children, just like Lily, whom she can dress in brightly colored flamenco dresses and whose soft skin and silky hair she can kiss and stroke as much as she wants when she tucks them in their beds at night by the star-speckled view from their curtainless window.

She thinks about all these things, and lets them run wild out of her private treasure box into the silence of the forest.

©

Charlotte walks into the kitchen. Beth is poring over a rabbit-and-mushroom pie recipe and listening to country-western music on the radio.

I bought some grapefruit juice as well. Charlotte takes the milk and grapefruit juice cartons out of her grocery bag and fits them next to the Coca-Cola bottle in the fridge.

Thank you so much.

It's a pretty little village, actually.

Aren't the cobbled pavements gorgeous?

Only I got stuck behind a sheep on the way.

Those loose sheep! I don't understand why Kevin Roberts doesn't look after his flock better. Beth touches Charlotte's shoulders and guides her to a chair. Sit down now. I'll make you a nice pot of tea.

Charlotte hesitates. She thinks about the daisy-patterned lace wrapped up in lilac tissue paper in her handbag and is dying to try it on. And then she remembers Lily.

Lily's outside playing hide-and-seek with the triplets, says Beth, sensing the awakening of Charlotte's anxiousness. I've told Amy to look after her properly from now on, so don't worry.

I'm not worrying, says Charlotte truthfully. Let me just nip up to the bathroom. I'll be down again in a minute.

Charlotte slips out the door and goes upstairs to the bedroom. She closes the door, takes off her cotton trousers and Marks & Spencer briefs, unwraps the thong, and carefully fits it on.

She stuffs the tissue paper in the bottom drawer of the chest and stands in front of the full-length mirror, tracing the lace against her flesh.

                                ○৯

Jude spies Amy's white T-shirt in the forest gloom behind the fence.

I can see you.

Amy doesn't move.

I can see you squatting in a ball in a dried-up stream by a foxhole.

Amy gets up, smiling, and stretches.

That was uncomfortable.

You're not supposed to hide in the forest, you know that. You know the forest's too big and I haven't got a torch on me.

That's why I hid at the edge.

We should have mentioned it before, sulks Jude. I bet Lily followed you and has got herself lost in the forest again.

Amy feels the same whoosh in the pit of her stomach.

She can't be far, she was just a little in front of me.

You pancake, Amy! Why didn't you stop her? If I can't find her, it's all your fault.

Jude climbs over the fence and stomps off into the forest.

⤴

Is that it? whispers Joseph, gently rubbing in circles with his index finger.

A little lower down, Nest whispers back. No—that's too far. Up a little bit. Stop. Right there. Yes.

Should I press harder?

No, that's fine. Stop talking. Just kiss me.

⤴

When Jude can't find Lily, she and Amy separate themselves with five avenues of trees between them and walk forward simultaneously into the darkness.

Lily! Amy shouts. Lily, come out, poppet, we've stopped playing hide-and-seek.

Lily! Jude shouts. Lily, come out at once!

After twenty minutes of searching without any luck, they run over to Sam, whom Jude found first of all and who has gone back to her bone-learning at the top of the tumulus.

Amy's lost Lily, says Jude. You've got to come help us find her.

Sam takes one last look at the bone name she always forgets, which she knows she'll be tested on, and repeats it over and over again in her head as she puts the book aside and rolls down the tumulus.

⌒

Beth dusts part of the table with flour, reaches for the lump of pastry dough, and kneads it on the table with her fingers. Squish it up, press it down and out. Squish it up, press it down and out. Her fingers caress the dough with mathematical precision.

She reaches for the rolling pin, rubs it in flour, and flattens the dough, losing herself in a faraway, hazy place where her heart beats fast and the hairs on her arms prickle with anticipation.

⌒

The triplets line up at the edge of the forest, five avenues apart, and decide to walk forward shouting Lily! every ten seconds and then listening. They head deep into the phalanx of softly rustling trees.

Lily! Tick. Tock. Tick. Tock. . . . Lily!

Fractured *Lily*s echo like mischievous, runaway Ping-Pong balls you can see but cannot catch.

The triplets emerge from the other side of the forest an hour later and look down on familiar landmarks from an unfamiliar angle. They see the chapel of Jacob Jones—the minister with tobacco breath, who comes more and more regularly to their house for Sunday lunch—surrounded by the gray splodges of gravestones, and colorful undershirts hanging in neat pairs on the clothesline behind the vicarage.

They walk along one edge of the forest to the far end and make their way back home through its other half. When they come out at the other end, they see Lily paddling in the stream, talking to herself.

Lily! Jude yells out. Where on earth have you been?

Lily looks straight ahead at the triplets' mud-flecked legs and then up at their identical hawkeyed expressions.

Having tea with the Mushroom Man, she answers. And toasted crumpets with creamy butter and pink marshmallow spread.

5

Before dinner, Amy knocks on Lily's door.

Come in.

Lily is lying on the floor, drawing a picture, her colored felt-tip pens scattered around her. Amy glances around the room; inhabited by other people and their belongings, it looks and smells different.

That's a pretty picture, Amy says. Lily has drawn a man with a beard, bobble hat, and cloak, sitting on a throne at a table. In front of him are a toolbox, some large bottles, mushroom-shaped molds, and what looks like a bowl of plums. In the background are a huge television set and winged creatures looking in through a window.

It's the Mushroom Man, Lily informs Amy, as if she hadn't already guessed.

Amy sits down alongside her.

I'm making him a present because he said he'd turn me into an invisible fairy tomorrow and I want to show him how grateful I am. Lily starts to color the man's beard gray.

Do you know how long we spent looking for you this afternoon? asks Amy.

Lily shakes her head. She puts the top on the gray felt-tip and reaches for the red to color the hat and the cloak.

More than two hours. We searched the whole forest. We couldn't find you anywhere. You worried us sick.

I told you, I was with the Mushroom Man.

But you were meant to be playing hide-and-seek.

I *was* playing hide-and-seek. I was hiding with the Mushroom Man.

Are you going to tell me where you were hiding with the Mushroom Man?

Of course not! Lily laughs. That would be breaking a promise to the Mushroom Man.

Amy watches Lily's unflinching face concentrate on her coloring.

Suit yourself, Amy says. She walks out of the room.

Any luck? Jude is hovering on the landing.

Amy shakes her head.

Didn't she say anything?

She said she would be breaking a promise to the Mushroom Man if she told me where she was hiding.

Jude rolls her eyes. I'll try.

Jude —

Don't worry, I'll be nice.

Jude bangs on Lily's door.

Come in.

Hi, Lily.

Hi, Jude.

Jude sits cross-legged opposite her. She stares at Lily's upside-down picture.

Do you like drawing? asks Jude.

Yes, answers Lily. I like it a lot.

Jude picks up the red felt-tip and starts coloring the nails of her left hand.

Lily, you know Amy made up that story, don't you?

Lily doesn't say anything. She starts drawing completed mush-room umbrellas at the end of the Mushroom Man's table.

Lily, you know the Mushroom Man and the fairies aren't for real, right?

You've just killed a fairy.

What?

It's in *Peter Pan*. Every time someone says they don't believe in fairies, a fairy dies.

But *Peter Pan* isn't for real either, silly.

Lily tries to snatch the red felt-tip out of Jude's hand. Don't waste it, Lily snaps. It's running out enough as it is.

Jude lets the pen go. Lily pulls at it too hard, and the point dives down at the picture, streaking a bright red line across it.

Now look what you've done. Lily bursts into tears.

Sorry, poppet.

You've ruined the Mushroom Man's thank-you present.

Thank-you present?

The Mushroom Man said he'd turn me into an invisible fairy tomorrow, and I wanted to give him a thank-you present. She's wailing loudly now.

Amy bursts into the room. What's going on?

I'll find you an even better present to give him, Jude assures Lily, disappearing through the doorway.

✍

I'm just not in the mood anymore, Beth says, noting Charlotte's untouched glass of red wine and pouring herself another. She looks out the open kitchen window at the fertile fuchsia sunset bleeding over everything, even into the forest. I used to like nothing better than losing myself in the color and texture of paint. Now I just feel guilty — guilty about not giving all my attention to the children, guilty about concentrating instead on perfecting a nonexistent person's eyebrow.

Charlotte remembers she has forgotten to pack her tweezers for plucking her eyebrows.

And it's frustrating, because everyone needs to do things like perfecting nonexistent people's eyebrows, but I can't, I feel guilty. I feel a tapping on my shoulder, Charlotte. I see a shaking of a head.

Charlotte has stopped listening to Beth's absurd talk of nonexistent eyebrows. She is too engrossed in thinking about what her own real, runaway eyebrows will look like by the end of the week: like the triplets'? like furry caterpillars?

Do you get this tapping on the shoulder, Charlotte? asks Beth. Tapping?

Guilt, says Beth. Charlotte's ears prick up. Do you ever feel guilt?

Charlotte certainly does have a lot to say about guilt. In particular she has a lot to say about Beth's guilt. But her own guilt? What guilt?

Not really, answers Charlotte. I don't think I've got anything to feel guilty about. I've always tried to do what I think is right. I've always tried to put others first.

There is a moment of quiet. Beth takes a gulp of wine and wonders if a sky can be any more beautiful.

Can a sky be any more beautiful? she asks Charlotte, moving toward the stove to check on the rabbit-and-mushroom pie.

It's a pretty sky.

Jude walks into her bedroom and sits beside Sam, who is lying on her bed: she is listening to her Walkman and playing Super Mario III on her Nintendo.

You're always playing on your Nintendo, Jude shouts.

Sam shrugs and carries on heading for a magic Super Mushroom to grow bigger and stronger.

You've got to help me think of a present for Lily's Mushroom Man, says Jude, right up against Sam's left ear, otherwise we're all in trouble.

Sam reluctantly removes her headphones, but continues staring at the Nintendo screen.

Lily was drawing this picture for him, and her pen slipped and streaked across the picture. She blamed me—you know the way little kids like to hit out on someone—and I said I'd find her an even better present for him. I didn't want her to go crying down to Auntie Charlotte and upsetting Mum.

The explosive sounds of Red Giant Koopa Troopas being zapped.

How old is he supposed to be?

Dunno. Old.

Ask Lily.

What?

Go and ask Lily, and then we'll know exactly what to give him.

Jude bangs on Lily's door.

Come in, says Lily. She is playing hangman with Amy.

How old is the Mushroom Man, Lily?

Jude! Amy frowns up at her. Lily looks suspicious.

Forty-five, Lily says cautiously. He's an old man.

Thank you, Lily. Jude walks out of the room and back to Sam.

———

Forty-five, states Jude, looking at the Nintendo screen and Super Mario in his frog suit swimming around in Water Land, preparing for a Blooper Nanny ambush.

Give her something of Dad's.

Dad's?

Dad was nearly forty-five when he died.

Jude walks out of the room back to Lily and Amy.

Mum said we could give something of Dad's.

Mum said *what?* demands Amy.

She did. She said Lily could have something of Dad's.

I don't believe you.

Go and ask her, challenges Jude, knowing that Amy won't go and ask her if she has said Go and ask her.

Jude wanders to the chest of drawers and rummages. She finds one of her dad's old Swiss Army knives and some lilac tissue paper with a sticker on it saying "With Best Wishes from the Little Welsh Bobbin Lace Shop." She shows them to Lily. Here you are. And I've even found some nice paper to wrap it up in.

Jude! Are you bananas? There's no way you're giving Lily a knife.

I like the knife, says Lily. And I'm not a baby, Amy. I'll be careful.

Of course Lily will be careful, Amy, says Jude. Amy is seething.

Lily wraps the knife in the tissue paper and then starts making a little thank-you card to go with it.

The rabbit-and-mushroom pie is an enormous success. The pastry is perfect, the rabbit is succulent, and the mushrooms are smooth and juicy. There are also carrots glazed in an orange-rind-and-brown-sugar sauce, and sweet new potatoes sprinkled with fresh parsley. And Beth has lit four tall white candles on the table, which make her best glazed plates shine like mother-of-pearl and everyone's face glow like that of a ghost.

Sam is talking about the gangster film they were watching the night before.

I'm not allowed to watch television, interrupts Lily. Mummy says it rots the brain.

The clinking of cutlery.

None at all? It's Nest. The words pop out before she can stop them. She stuffs a potato in her mouth to stop anything else from popping out.

Daddy and Pavlova sometimes let me watch it on Tuesday and Thursday evenings when Mummy's at her yoga class. Charlotte swallows hard and tries to catch Lily's eye. Lily is purposely addressing Nest. But it's only usually the news then. Even if I do catch a cartoon or a fun show, it's always at the tail end, when the baddies have been caught or the presenter is saying good-bye and announcing all the fun things that will happen in the next show, which I won't be able to watch.

Come on now, darling, Charlotte says. Mummy takes you to the cinema.

You took me once to the cinema to see *Fantasia,* which was all classical music, Lily clarifies, sticking her fork into a fat mushroom bit.

Beth pats her hands down on the table as if to dot a full stop.

Who wants custard with their rhubarb turnover cake? asks Beth. And who likes their custard extra sweet?

⟨◈⟩

WE HUNGRIE AND NO HOME.

PLEASE GIVE DALMATIONS.

THANK YOU.

These are the words written on the cardboard strip held by a little Albanian Gypsy boy sitting on his mother's lap near the bottom of an escalator in the Oxford Circus tube station. Preoccupied people with shopped-out feet and shampoo-smelling hair swish past, not reading the sign, but occasionally dropping a coin in the Pot Noodle container without looking back.

Pavlova steps onto the escalator and feasts her eyes on the diagonal of theater advertisements slipping slowly past her. When she reaches the bottom, she turns her head and sees the cardboard sign, sees the cut on the Gypsy boy's forehead, sees the mother's long braids. She reads the sign.

She steps onto nonmoving ground, walks over to them, takes out a pen from her rucksack. She tries to explain that there are spelling mistakes. She tries to take the cardboard out of the boy's grip so that she can turn it over and write a new message. But the boy starts to cry and the mother looks suspicious.

Pavlova takes out her purse. She takes out half of what remains of the money Richard gave her this morning, notes—the kind of money she is sure the boy and his mother have never seen before—folds them neatly together, and presses them into the mother's hand. She scuttles away without looking back.

At the platform, she buys a copy of *Vogue* from the newsstand, and a Cadbury's Wispa Gold bar.

Charlotte is throwing up in the bathroom. You can hear the retching throughout the house.

Beth knocks on the door. Lily is behind her.

Is there anything I can get you, Charlotte dear?

Retch. Up it comes again.

I'm okay. Just leave me be.

Are you all right, Mummy? asks Lily, worried.

Mummy's fine. Just leave me be.

Beth takes Lily by the hand. Come away, pet. Mummy will be fine. Just an upset stomach. We all get it, once in a while. Why don't we go and find you a nice book to read?

Can I watch television?

Beth hesitates. All right, then. We'll see what's on.

❧

Mr. Newman picks up the telephone receiver and calls Pavlova's cell phone.

It's her voice mail. He leaves a message.

It's me. Just ringing to ask what time you'll be back. I suppose I'll see you later. Okay, bye. He puts the receiver down.

He picks the receiver up again and calls Charlotte's cell phone.

It's her voice mail. He leaves a message.

It's me. Hope you got out of that sheep — ho ho ho. I suppose I'll speak to you later. Have fun. Bye. He puts the receiver down.

He looks out the window at two children trying out their new skateboard.

❧

Lily knocks on the bathroom door during a commercial break.

Are you feeling better, Mummy?

Come in here a second, Lily.

Lily unlatches the door into the vinegar smell of sick and her mother crouching over the toilet, her hair tied off her pale face in a ponytail.

Close the door. Lily closes the door. We're going home tomorrow, Charlotte informs her. Mummy's not well and I don't like it here.

I like it here. Please can we stay here, Mummy. Please. Please.

Sorry, Lily. Charlotte blows her nose.

Please —

And I want you to start packing your things tonight.

-⁂◯

I don't want children, announces Nest. Joseph is walking her home across the patchwork of fields and around the marsh with duck nests, which used to be a lake. Once you've got them, you're stuck with them. It's not as if you can put them aside for a while and then come back to them when you're more in the mood.

Of course not, says Joseph.

And however much you give them, they'll always find something to moan about. They'll always have problems. It will always be the mother's fault.

And the father's.

But it isn't. For some reason it's never the father's fault. It's always the mother. The poor knackered mother who puts their meals on the table, washes their dirty underwear, empties the wastepaper bins in their bedrooms, deals with most of the crap.

Won't you feel empty — not having any children?

Because I've never had some brat-to-be swelling in my belly? Nest laughs.

Joseph feels disgusted. He can't believe his softness is speaking like this.

No, I won't feel empty, Nest says. I'll feel free.

They get to the boundary line. Nest unbuckles Joseph's belt, undoes the button at the top of his jeans, unzips his fly. His jeans fall down his legs to form a puddle around his shoes. She pulls down his stripy boxer shorts and starts licking between his legs. He weaves his fingers into her silky hair, feels himself getting a hard-on, and stares absently ahead at the discoloring nightfall.

ii

Lily glances at the clock on the bedside table: six o'clock — the hands are one smooth black line pointing at opposite ends. She turns to check on her mother: She is sleeping, face upward, hair still tied off her face in a ponytail, a sick-bowl on the bedside table near her. Lily thinks of a gone-wrong Sleeping Beauty before slipping out of bed and out the door and opening the airing cupboard, where she has hidden the clothes Amy gave her yesterday morning, a clean pair of her own socks and panties, and the Mushroom Man's thank-you card and present.

She tiptoes to the bathroom to change. She pulls on her own frilly panties and polka-dotted socks, Joseph's Ninja Turtles shorts, Jude's Kellogg's Coco Pops T-shirt, and Amy's hand-knitted, yellow sweater.

She tiptoes down the stairs and into the kitchen, breaks off a banana from the bunch in the fruit bowl, and tiptoes to the porch to put on her red Wellingtons.

She opens the door and runs down the slope toward the forest.

6

My little girl, she's vanished. . . . Anything between five and eleven hours . . . Another two hours! Can't they come around any sooner than that? . . . How can a mother whose only daughter has disappeared off the face of the earth possibly keep calm?

Charlotte slams the phone down. Her tiny frame quakes. She weeps. She properly weeps.

Beth wraps her arms around her sister and hugs her close. She kisses her hair, which still smells of sick, and her wet, warm, salty cheeks. For the first time, Beth feels close to her sister.

Shall we call Richard? asks Beth.

✧

Mr. Newman is watching Pavlova marinate the pork chops they are having for dinner. He watches her crack open two eggs into a glass bowl, crush a clove of garlic, add three pinches of curry powder, and beat the mixture with a fork, holding the glass bowl tight against her chest.

The telephone rings. Mr. Newman ignores it. A beep. The answering machine plays Charlotte's panicked message aloud.

Lily's gone missing, Richard. . . . We can't find her anywhere. . . . I'm worried sick. . . . Call me back as soon as you get this.

I'm sure it's nothing to be concerned about, says Mr. Newman. She probably just went for a walk and got lost. And little kids, they've got no concept of time—especially Lily.

Lily's my little cutie, says Pavlova.

Mr. Newman smiles. Pavlova turns around and starts stabbing the pork chops with a skewer on the chopping board.

Bang. Bang. Bang. Bang.

❧

Amy flings open the rusty gate—which moans, hits itself hard against the wall, and creaks halfway closed—runs down the snaking front garden path, through the shadows of a cluster of firs, and hammers on the door with the cross-shaped metal knocker.

Mr. Jones! Amy shouts. Mr. Jones, open up! Mr. Jones!

Only the hissing of the firs behind her in the breeze, and the silence of the higgledy-piggledy shape of the vicarage choking in ivy.

She walks slowly back up the path—repeatedly looking behind— excuses herself past the half-open gate, and speeds to a jog past the small graveyard toward the chapel. As she gets closer, she hears the sharp shocks of organ chords.

~ᡚ

Thanks for looking, says Joseph.

It's the least we can do, son, replies Nest's father. His face is leathery and weather-beaten, and his hands are clownishly big. Let us know if you need any more help.

If you could just keep an eye out.

Aye, we'll certainly do that.

Joseph heads for the door. Nest follows him.

Are you two not staying for dinner, then? calls out Nest's mother, who has white hairs spurting out from the moles on her face and who lugs her enormous breasts around like two permanent, overdue pregnancies.

I've made some nice venison stew, and a barrel of fresh ale arrived from Carmarthen today.

I'd best be heading back, answers Joseph. Thanks all the same, Mrs. Thomas.

And I suppose you're going with him, madame. Nest nods. We hardly see you at all these days.

I'll be back tomorrow, Mam. Nest slams the door.

Young and in love. Nest's father chuckles and gives his wife a quick peck on the cheek. Young and in love, Sarah.

❦

Mr. Jones is preparing the altar for the Sunday-evening service. He looks up.

Jude!

It's Amy, Mr. Jones.

So sorry, Am—

Mr. Jones, you have to help us. My six-year-old cousin Lily's gone missing. I have a feeling it's serious. I have to speak to you in private.

Mr. Jones nods gravely in his ministerial way and leads Amy by the hand to the baptistery, which is cut off and quiet and where the midafternoon sun spills in through the petal-shaped windows. They sit down next to each other in a corner, on the stone slab seating that juts out from the wall. The organ music is quieter here. Only the faint splashing sound of a drunk wasp drowning in the shallow water of the font.

Amy, Mr. Jones invites. She notices that today he smells more of musty old clothes than tobacco.

Amy explains how Lily is staying on their farm with their auntie Charlotte, how Lily has gone missing before, how Lily became obsessed with a fairy tale Amy herself made up about a Mushroom Man.

I have a feeling she won't come back this time, she confides. I have a permanent whoosh in the pit of my stomach. I have a feeling . . . She hesitates. I have a feeling, Mr. Jones, and I know it sounds ridiculous . . .

Nothing will sound ridiculous to me.

I have a feeling the Mushroom Man has turned Lily into an invisible fairy.

Mr. Jones coughs. An invisible fairy?

I have a feeling the story I made up about the Mushroom Man is true. I have a feeling there are powers out there which people don't realize. That's why I came to you, because you believe in divine powers and the angel Gabriel and things. I thought you might be able to give me a hint on how to get Lily back.

Mr. Jones scratches his balding scalp.

Lily told us that she saw the Mushroom Man when she was alone in the forest, that he's got a belly from drinking too much fairy plum juice, that she had tea with him, and toasted crumpets with creamy butter and pink marshmallow spread. Yesterday evening she told us that the Mushroom Man was going to turn her into an invisible fairy today. She was going to bring him a thank-you present.

How long has Lily been missing for, Amy?

Anything between five and eleven hours. The amused twinkle in Mr. Jones's eye suddenly metamorphoses into a squint. When Auntie Charlotte woke up this morning at ten o'clock, Lily wasn't in the double bed beside her. But she was still in bed at five o'clock in the morning, when Auntie Charlotte went to sleep after being sick all night.

Have you seen anyone unusual in the forest, Amy?

Amy cocks her head and looks up at the star of Bethlehem in the middle of the stained-glass skyline. No, I don't think so. But that doesn't mean anything, Mr. Jones. These fairy people only approach a special few.

We'll have a quick look around the fields near here, then I'll drop you back home in the car, and then I'll come around again straight after the evening service if you still haven't found her.

I can walk back on my own, Mr. Jones.

I'd rather make sure you got home safely, Amy. He tries to sound cheerful.

༄

Beth and Charlotte have been ranging the moors in Beth's clapped-out Ford, leaving Jude and Sam to stay in the farmhouse in case Lily returns. It is drizzling. The windshield wipers screech, bowing and rising obediently. The car bumps uncomfortably along the tracks and over the cattle grids, and the moors are an endless, featureless face of uncontrollable heather with big scabs of lichen-licked rocks.

She can't be here, declares Charlotte.

It isn't impossible, answers Beth.

They drive into yet another web of tracks, until a thickening mist silently shoos them away.

༄

Any luck? Sam asks, as soon as Amy walks into the kitchen. You were ages.

Amy shakes her head. Any news your end?

Nothing, Sam sighs. Mum and Auntie Charlotte have taken the car up to the moors. The police are coming in an hour.

Police? Amy wonders what good any uniformed people with helmets and clipboards could do for someone who's been turned into an invisible fairy. She walks to the cupboard and takes out the tin of hot chocolate powder. Who wants hot chocolate? Jude and Sam both raise their hands.

I went to see Mr. Jones, Amy explains, as she pours milk into a saucepan on the hob and adds three fragile mountains of chocolate powder with a serving spoon. I reckoned he might be one to believe me if I told him I thought Lily had been turned into an invisible fairy by the Mushroom Man.

You're sick, Jude snipes. This is no time for joking about even further with your dumb fairy tale when it was your dumb fairy tale that was responsible for Lily going missing twice before and probably this time too.

Jude, Sam intervenes.

I know, it's my fault, Amy sobs, stirring teardrops into the frothing hot chocolate. And I know that Lily might never come back to us if we don't think of a clever plan soon.

⋅✒○

Mr. Newman stares at the shape of Pavlova's pert bum cheeks and hears the sizzling and popping of the pork chops in the frying pan.

He gets up, licks his right index finger, shoves his hand up her miniskirt and into her panties, and sticks his finger hard up her bumhole.

Ouch! Pavlova yelps, nearly knocking over the frying pan.

Sorry, fruitcake. He wiggles out his hand and strokes her hair.

I'm not into that end, Pavlova says firmly.

That's another reason I don't want to have children, resumes Nest, as she walks up the slope to the house, holding Joseph's hand. If something bad happened to one of them, it would totally destroy me.

There's a risk with everything.

But we're talking children here, not things. We're talking half of ourselves.

You always have to twist everything.

That's so unfair, Josie. She tugs on his arm. I'm just trying to be practical.

7

We just want to get the facts straight before we act upon anything, says Police Officer Number One, who looks identical to Police Officer Number Two except for a bigger belly.

Charlotte sits at the end of the table, as withered as a plant without water.

The police officers establish Lily's appearance, approximately what time she went missing, the clothes she must have been wearing.

Did she take anything with her? A cuddly toy, perhaps? inquires Police Officer Number Two.

She doesn't have any cuddly toys, replies Charlotte.

Police Officer Number Two exchanges looks with Police Officer Number One and writes on his notepad on his clipboard. Amy and Jude have sheepish expressions.

So as far as you know, she was empty-handed? asks Police Officer

Number One. Charlotte nods. Beth nods. Police Officer Number One turns to the children and raises his eyebrows at them as if they aren't worthy of speech.

Well, actually . . . I know she took a thank-you card . . . and present for a fairy-tale character she was fascinated by, Amy stumbles. Police Officer Number One raises his eyebrows even higher. Charlotte's already beady eyes now threaten to pop out of their sockets.

Which fairy-tale character? quizzes Police Officer Number Two.

Someone I made up called the Mushroom Man, Amy mumbles. I told Lily that there is a man called the Mushroom Man who is a friend of the fairies and makes them umbrellas—*mushrooms*—and that the fairies have made him invisible like them.

That's so cool! exclaims Nest. The words jack-in-the-box out again before she can stop them. She feels the blood rushing to her ears.

The police officers write "Mushroom Man" on their notepads and underline it.

But why a thank-you card and present? presses Police Officer Number One.

She said he was going to turn her into an invisible fairy today, Amy stammers. She said she wanted to show that she was grateful.

And what present did Lily take for this Mushroom Man? presses Police Officer Number Two.

Amy looks at Jude, who is purposefully looking in the other direction, and then at her mother, who she thought knew about it but who appears as blank as a switched-off television screen. She feels as if her stomach is going to explode with whooshes.

One of Dad's Swiss Army knives, Amy blurts. Charlotte gasps.

The police officers glumly write "Swiss Army knife" below "Mushroom Man."

Where on earth did she get that from? Beth demands.

Jude gave it to her, Amy says, on the verge of tears. She found it in your chest of drawers. She said you said Lily could have it.

Me? Beth retorts.

Sorry, says Jude.

Jude! Beth and Amy exclaim together.

Just a Swiss Army knife? Police Officer Number Two probes.

Yes, as far as I know, Amy replies. And she made a little card to go with it and wrapped it in some purple tissue paper we also found in the chest of drawers.

Purple tissue paper that had a sticker on it saying "With Best Wishes from the Little Welsh Bobbin Lace Shop," clarifies Jude.

That tissue paper isn't mine, Beth muses out loud. Charlotte feels she is in hell.

The police officers write everything down neatly with their black pens.

⁓◌

I want to get you a special gift, says Mr. Newman, hoping to compensate for his naughty impulse, which didn't go down well and which might sabotage the prospect of gymnastic sex after dinner. Can you suggest something, my beauty? His ulterior motive is as obvious to Pavlova as dirty footprints on a cream carpet. She makes the most of it.

There are these earrings . . . , she begins in mock coyness, carefully arranging the fried mushrooms on top of the pork chops on their plates. They're these little diamond studs from Tiffany's . . .

⟡

You mentioned Lily went missing once before, recalls Police Officer Number One, turning to Charlotte.

She went missing yesterday morning, sniffles Charlotte. The triplets can tell you more about that.

Police Officer Number One turns to the triplets and does the same raising of the eyebrows.

Actually she went missing *twice* before, Sam chirps up. Beth rests her hand on Charlotte's shoulder, which is on the verge of going into spasm. She went missing in the morning when we went mushroom picking, and she went missing in the afternoon when we were playing hide-and-seek.

And where did you find her? asks Police Officer Number Two.

We found her both times in the stream at the edge of the forest.

Did she say where she had been?

She said both times that she had been with the Mushroom Man.

Charlotte breaks down into hysterical sobbing. Beth hugs her tight and makes soft hushing sounds.

Police Officer Number One clears his throat and straightens his jacket, preparing for serious business.

Now, I want you all to think very carefully about this next question, he begins. Have you seen anyone strange on the farm recently?

How old's your sister? asks Mr. Newman, tucking into his pork chop.

Twenty-five, answers Pavlova. She's two years older, she's called Tatiana, and she works in a bakery. Mr. Newman pictures a big blonde in a white paper hat and an apron covered in flour, placing sticky cherries on little white-icing fairy cakes, and stores the image for a rainy day.

Do you get on well?

Not really. Pavlova shrugs. We have different interests. She gets excited about carpets and matching curtains for the new flat she's bought with her husband.

What does her husband do?

He works in a condom factory.

There's a loud knock on the door. Beth excuses herself and goes out of the kitchen to the porch. She yanks open the stiff door.

Jacob!

Amy came to me this afternoon, he bursts out. Beth's eyes flit down to his mouth and then back up. She told me your six-year-old niece was missing. I was wondering whether I could be of any assistance.

That's very kind of you, Jacob, but I think the police are taking care of everything for the time being. She touches her hair. I would invite you in, it's just that at the moment the police are questioning us about it—

No, no, I didn't come for entertainment, Beth. Just to let you know that I'm there if you need anything.

That's very kind of you.

I'm just a telephone call away, he points out, walking off.

Thank you. Beth waves after him, feeling a peculiar concoction of pity and longing.

The sky is a whirl-wash of grays, and it has begun to spit. She closes the door.

Charlotte peers out the window and sees a strange man who looks uncannily similar to *him* glance back twice at the house as he shuffles away. She notices Beth's flushed face when she returns to the kitchen.

I'm going to call a few of my men to come and look around the farm with a couple of sniffer dogs as soon as they can get here, Police Officer Number One informs Beth and Charlotte, his back turned to the children. If we don't have any luck this evening, I'll send out a full search party first thing tomorrow morning, with a helicopter.

Go straight ahead and use our phone, says Beth.

I'd be much obliged, Mrs. Griffiths, replies Police Officer Number One. Our cellular phones don't seem to be picking up any reception here.

Can I make you some tea or coffee? Beth asks the officers.

Tea would be most welcome over here, answers Police Officer Number One, eyeing the half-eaten rhubarb turnover cake through the glass bowl covering it on the sideboard. With milk and three sugars.

Police Officer Number Two is looking over his notes. I'm all right, thank you.

⁊○

And your father, does he work in the condom factory too? asks Mr. Newman with a deadpan face, eager to see if he can flesh out even further the hilarious detail that Pavlova's brother-in-law works in a condom factory: a delicious and safe (he knows it's not sensible to let on about the fucking business) anecdote for the all-boys banter at his club.

He's too preoccupied with booze and sluts to get his arse out of bed at six in the morning to work in a factory, humphs Pavlova. As far as I know, he works in a bar in Tallinn, but I haven't had any contact with him since he walked out of the flat ten years ago. Good riddance, frankly—he was never interested in me or my sister, and he treated my mum like shit. She's still got the scars to prove it.

That's terrible.

⁊○

It's bucketing. Relentlessly. Sheets of heavy rain and hail propelled by forceful gusts of wind sting the seven police officers, the triplets,

Joseph and Nest, and the two Alsatian sniffer dogs, all of them dotting the fields being quickly embraced by night.

Beth is in the bathroom tending to Charlotte, who has just thrown up again.

I've got to go out and look for Lily, Charlotte mutters, pulling the chain and trying to stand up.

You're in no fit state, says Beth firmly.

I have to go find my little lost princess.

Just look at the weather and how dark it is. And there are enough people searching already.

I can't — I can't just stay inside when my baby's missing! Charlotte is hysterical.

Well, I'm not letting you go anywhere.

You bitch, I hate you. I hate your farm. I hate your children, who have made Lily go missing.

It's not the children's fault, chokes Beth.

It is! It is! Charlotte chants like a child in a tantrum. And it's your fault too, for making us come here.

꩜

The scent's dead, Police Officer Number One informs Beth and Charlotte as he stands dripping in the doorway. The dogs don't seem to be picking up on anything, and the wind and rain aren't helping. We did our best to search the fields and forest, but no sign, I'm afraid.

My baby! whimpers Charlotte.

We'll have to leave it there for tonight, but we'll be back first thing tomorrow morning with a larger team and more dogs, and there'll also be a helicopter.

You can't just go! Charlotte blubbers.

There's nothing more we can do at this stage, I'm afraid, Mrs. Newman. He touches the top of his hat and bows his head — more like a circus performer than a policeman.

Until tomorrow, then, ladies. He waddles off.

Charlotte stamps her foot. You can't just piss off to catch last orders at your local pub when a tiny child's life is in danger, she yells after him.

Police Officer Number One keeps walking.

Beth tries to pull Charlotte from the door. You mustn't behave like that to someone who's trying to help us, Charlotte.

Don't you dare teach me how to behave, Charlotte rages. You who can't stop touching up all the dirty men in this godforsaken place.

Pardon?

I saw the look of that man who came when the police officers were here. I saw your guilty face.

Do you mean Mr. Jones? He's our local minister.

As if that would ever stop you! That's why you're damned, Beth. That's why your husband and your dogs die on you and your children are evil. You don't give a shit. You just don't give a shit.

Beth turns away, tears streaming down her cheeks; sour tears streaming away with the possibility of reconciliation and friendship.

Beth runs into the front field in her huge green mackintosh, having secretly locked Charlotte, who is throwing up again, in the bathroom. She takes out the whistle with which she used to order her sheepdog around and blows it hard.

The blue and orange mackintoshed blobs by the stream, which are almost dissolved into the darkness, turn around. Beth gestures to them with big arm movements to come back, blowing again and again with her whistle and yelling as hard as she can against the wind and rain that are slapping her face.

The children obediently walk up the slope toward the house.

8

They don't eat dinner together. Beth, Joseph, and Nest are in the studio, examining a local map and establishing who will search where. The triplets are in the kitchen, sitting on the counter and crunching on cream crackers and cheese. Charlotte is in the bathroom, still throwing up, not yet aware that she has been locked in.

You can't go looking on your own, Mum, says Joseph. Nest should go with you instead of me. He gently squeezes Nest's hand. She nods.

I'll be fine, answers Beth. I'll take Dad's shotgun.

The shotgun! Joseph is horrified—his mother's suggestion is absurdly uncharacteristic. You've never touched that thing in your life. You wouldn't know how to use it.

As if I would ever use it!

Then what's the point?

It's a threat, asserts Beth, not quite recognizing the sound of her own voice. And a threat like that should be enough to scare anyone away.

So you think — says Nest.

I don't think anything, dear, Beth interrupts. But it's best to take precautions.

ॐ

Jude finds it hard to admit, but she's starting to be persuaded by Amy's conviction that Lily really *did* meet the Mushroom Man in the forest the two times she said she did and that the Mushroom Man has turned her into an invisible fairy. Jude weighs it up and demands, Well, what else? They've searched everywhere, and they know the landscape as intimately as the features on their mother's face. Jude weighs it up and demands, And kidnappers don't come kidnapping on a farm in the middle of the countryside, do they?

Sam is starting to be persuaded too. Sam weighs it up and muses, If there can be worlds with Red Giant Koopa Troopas and Blooper Nannies in a tiny plastic Nintendo, then what's there to argue against simple fairy worlds in the trees? Sam weighs it up and muses, If people weren't aware of the existence of the millions of eight-legged dust mites crawling around in their beds until the discovery of the microscope, then what's there to argue against the existence of millions of worlds we don't have the technology yet to fathom?

Jude demands and Sam muses and Amy bangs on and on about it. And they all drop cream-cracker and cheese crumbs on the floor, debating with full mouths about it.

⌒

Charlotte thumps on the bathroom door. I'm locked in! I'm locked in! Let me out! Let me out!

Beth, Joseph, and Nest hear it, but pretend not to hear it. The triplets hear it, can't help laughing about it, and don't do anything about it. They have all put Charlotte aside for a while, like an awkward piece of homework.

Charlotte hears voices from downstairs and knows that they can hear her too. She knows that this is a conspiracy, and she feels hatred thick and black and scorching like a cauldron of gluey tar. She calls Beth's children the devil's offspring and spits and rants and raves and curses.

Beth picks up the telephone receiver and punches in Mr. Newman's number.

⌒

Mr. Newman is drinking wine and puffing on a cigar, leering at Pavlova and feeling well fed.

The telephone rings. Mr. Newman ignores it. A beep. The answering machine records Beth's message out loud.

Richard, it's Beth. Charlotte's hysterical and I don't know what to do. We're all very worried—Lily's been missing for at least ten hours now, and the police haven't had any luck in finding her. Please ring me right back as soon as you get this message.

Mr. Newman snatches up the telephone receiver and calls Beth right back. Beth, it's Richard, I'd no idea she'd been gone that long. . . . And the police? . . . Oh, God . . . I'm coming to you . . . I'm going to have to wait half an hour or so because I've had a bit to drink, but I'm coming to you as soon as I can.

He slams the receiver down. He puts out his cigar. He pushes away Pavlova, who is stroking his balding scalp consolingly. He goes to the sink, fills himself a large mug of water, and informs Pavlova without looking at her that he has to go find his daughter.

He hurries out of the kitchen and goes upstairs for a shower to sober himself up.

☙

Uncle Richard will be here around midnight, Beth informs the triplets. I hope to be back to let him into the house myself, but I'd like one of you to stay awake until I return, just in case.

The triplets assure her they'll all stay awake. They watch their mother, Joseph, and Nest fit fresh batteries into flashlights, zip themselves up in big mackintoshes, and step into green Wellingtons. They watch their mother open the cabinet and take out their father's old shotgun. They wave their mother, Joseph, and Nest off and wish them well.

Lock the door after us, Beth shouts back. Both the bottom and top locks.

Suddenly the house feels bereft. Charlotte has stopped screaming, and a stillness lingers like a bad smell. Sam locks the front door and shakes it to make sure that it is firmly shut.

If someone's been made invisible, declares Jude, then they're as good as dead to us.

Not at all, snaps Amy. We just have to work harder to communicate with them, that's all. We just have to use our imagination a bit.

Have you communicated with Lily? asks Jude, trying to sound casual.

Amy shakes her head. Not yet. We have to find her first.

How on earth are we going to find someone who's invisible?

By exactly the same methods we would use to search for someone who isn't invisible, answers Amy.

Where would we start?

In the forest, of course, says Amy. Because I'm pretty sure the fairies have taken Lily to one of their tree palaces. Why don't we all go down there now?

~⌀

Beth is enraged. Beth is enraged because this is her land and her heart and her magic and it has been violated. She won't admit it to the children or to her hysterical sister, but she suspects an impostor. She suspects someone entered into her lush fields. She suspects that someone abducted Lily.

Beth is petrified. Beth is petrified because she reads the papers and watches the news and knows that abducted children don't usually come back. She is petrified because she knows that if Lily doesn't come back, the children will be devastated. She is petrified because she knows that if Lily doesn't come back, it will kill Charlotte. She is petrified because she knows that if Lily doesn't come back, she herself will be gnawed by guilt. Imperishable, implacable, venomous guilt.

So Beth is tramping across her fields, flashing a gun, which she doesn't know how to use, to let that someone know they're playing with fire. To let that someone know they can't take advantage of a single mother.

※

Mr. Newman zips down the motorway in his BMW with its personalized license plates reading "RICH" and sees everything in perspective. He feels a shit for mucking around with his daughter's au pair, whom he'll have to dismiss now. He feels a shit for deceiving his wife and neglecting his daughter and not going with them to his sister-in-law's. All he wants is to be strolling along in the park, talking about "Jack and the Beanstalk"—one arm around Charlotte's slight waist, the other holding Lily on his shoulders—or playing Snakes and Ladders with Lily on the kitchen table while Charlotte cooks her special fat-free paella behind them.

Mr. Newman zips down the motorway and sees families with bicycles atop their cars driving in the opposite direction, driving home from fun family weekends. He switches the radio off, overtakes the car in front of him, and heads toward the rain clouds.

⁓◌

The triplets hug the hedgerow, crouching down and moving quietly like a band of ambushers. They don't want to be spotted by their mother or Joseph or Nest, who will send them back to the house. Their hearts throb with clandestine adventure and the prospect of a fairy world with a Mushroom Man and an invisible Lily.

They cross the stream and climb the fence into the forest. It is pitch black. Jude and Sam switch on their flashlights.

There's no point using torches when Lily's invisible, says Amy. It's better to walk and look and listen and feel in the darkness.

Feel for cold spirit patches? asks Jude.

Shouldn't spirits be warm? Sam inquires.

Lily isn't a spirit, corrects Amy, because she's not dead. She's an invisible fairy, which is different.

I'm sure invisible fairies feel just the same as spirits, Jude huffs.

Of course they don't, Amy retorts. That's like saying humans feel the same as polar bears. Spirits and invisible fairies are different species.

How do invisible fairies feel, then, smarty-pants? Jude challenges.

You'll just *know* if you feel one—like you just *know* the feeling of falling in love when it hits you, even if it hasn't hit you before.

What do you know about falling in love? asks Jude. Unless

you count your one-sided crush on Felipe, who is always looking at me and who always saves all his tutti-frutti-flavored Jelly Bellies for me.

He probably gets you mixed up with Amy, Sam says curtly, glimpsing Amy's shattered face.

He knows I'm Jude, he calls me Jude all the time. I've told him about the beauty spot above my right eyebrow.

Charlotte opens the bathroom window, sticks her head out into the rain, and looks down—her long, thick, tangled hair hanging down like Rapunzel's. The distance to the ground beneath her—a hard stone patio—is greater than she envisaged, and the wall is a smooth vertical cliff of gray stone.

She closes the window and slumps back to the floor near the toilet. She feels weak and sick and dizzy and shivery and no longer has the energy to cry. Charlotte thinks about happiness and the way it is always cut off from her. Although she always does her best to stick to the rules, someone always comes with a big pair of scissors and puts an end to it.

Joseph and Nest aren't holding hands. They walk a few yards apart and shine their flashlights in opposite directions. Two restless golden circles that rarely meet slither over nature in its nighttime nakedness, licking it up in perfect cut-out circles.

Joseph and Nest feel important and responsible and grown-up, and they wear these new feelings like a dashing but slightly oversized new suit. Their minds are full of maps and policemen and helicopters, and they want to play their roles well.

◦

Amy walks straight into a tree trying to feel for an invisible Lily and bangs her head hard. Her head pounds and pounds and pounds, and she sees colored dots swimming through the air, and trees growing fatter one out of another. She flops to the ground.

Amy! Sam and Jude gasp. They rush over to her, and Sam starts performing mouth-to-mouth resuscitation as she has seen on television.

Amy regains consciousness almost immediately. Urghh! She pushes a three-headed Sam away and wipes her mouth. Then the pounding returns, relentless waves smashing against an isolated rock in the middle of the ocean. My head's cracking, she says.

Sam and Jude carry her awkwardly back to the house — Sam holding Amy's upper body, Jude the lower. Jude is crying and apologizing for what she said about Felipe before, saying that of course Felipe doesn't save all his tutti-frutti-flavored Jelly Bellies for her, that of course she hasn't told him about the beauty spot above her right eyebrow, that of course he can't tell her apart from Amy or

Sam. Jude cries and apologizes and wants to make amends so that Amy does not die with the last memory of her as being spiteful.

Amy does not say anything. She closes her eyes and pretends she is at death's door, and enjoys listening to Jude's uncharacteristic fawning.

9

Mr. Newman walks in through the half-open front door. Hello! he calls out. It's Richard. He walks cautiously into, across, and out of the kitchen, past the living room, past Beth's studio, and stands at the bottom of the stairs. Hello! he calls out again. He hears a faint scuttling noise and then a piercing, wild Help! Help!

Charlotte is beating on the bathroom door with her fist. Up here. Help! Help!

Mr. Newman bolts up the stairs. Puffed out, he stands shaking the closed door. Charlotte, is that you?

Richard, they've locked me in. Her voice is gruff and desperate. They're mad, Richard. They've locked me in.

Calm down, darling. He feels extremely uneasy. He has never heard his wife like this before, and there is nothing he can do. Do you know where the key is?

Hell, how would I know? she groans.

Do you know where Beth and the children have gone?

I've been locked in here without anyone speaking to me since this evening.

Are they outside looking for Lily?

Hell, how would I know? she repeats.

Try to stay calm.

Richard, she spits, I've been locked in the bathroom like an animal, and our daughter could well have been abducted. How can I possibly keep calm?

I'm going to look for them.

Don't leave me, please. She panics. Please stay here, Richard, I'm scared.

I won't leave you, he assures her. He sits down in front of the closed door. I'm right here.

He feels sick with the full recognition of his selfishness and foolishness and deceptiveness and licentiousness. His failure as a husband and a father and an upright man.

⁂

Pavlova is cleaning the dirty pans. She scrubs hard at the burnt fat, but it clings stubbornly to the stainless steel. She gives up, leaving the pans to soak overnight in soapy water, and takes off her yellow gloves.

Pavlova has never felt so empty: Pavlova might hate Charlotte — the way she sits primly in the drawing room with her electric foot

massager, reading *Good Housekeeping* and ordering Pavlova to make
her mint tea in a china cup with half a spoon of honey. Pavlova might
be repelled by Mr. Newman—the way he sticks his finger up her
arse when she's in the middle of cooking and the way he wants her
to call his insatiable dick all kinds of ridiculous names during fore-
play. But Pavlova adores Lily—the way she always says, Thank
you, Pavlova, that was most delicious, after every mealtime; the
way she sticks her tongue out and wiggles her bottom behind
her parents' backs; the way she talks about fairy-tale characters as
if they are her good friends. Lily reminds Pavlova of waking up in
the morning when she went camping with her mother and sister
the week after their father left them, of fresh air and the sight of
her mother boiling milk and frying eggs and potato slices over a
camp stove.

Pavlova isn't religious—though she does go to mass on Christmas
Eve—but she now says a prayer. She kneels on the Chinese rug in
the drawing room by the Steinway, on which Lily is learning to play,
and whispers in Estonian, Dear Lord, please don't let anything bad
have happened to little Lily. Amen. She makes the sign of the cross
across her face and chest.

⁂

Richard! Beth exclaims, flustered, about to put the shotgun back in
the hallway cabinet.

Mr. Newman stares at the gun and then past Beth's shoulder
at two identical-looking children carrying a third identical-looking

child, who seems to be unconscious, into the kitchen. Beth whips herself around to face the triplets.

Call an ambulance! Jude shouts. Amy's dying.

Beth shoves the gun into Mr. Newman's arms and rushes to Amy. She hadn't noticed the triplets, who approached the house a short distance behind her.

I'm okay, Amy says, trying to stand up in her still-spinning world. I just banged my head.

She could be bleeding internally, says Sam. Jude shivers.

How on earth did this happen? Beth guides Amy to a chair and examines her bruised forehead.

She bumped into a tree, says Jude. We were looking for Lily.

I thought I told you all to stay in the house.

Sorry, they all say in unison.

Beth goes to the freezer and takes out some ice, which she wraps in a tea towel and holds to Amy's forehead. Sam and Jude look up and, seeing the tall man with a gun in the doorway, let out ear-splitting screams.

I'm your uncle Richard, says Mr. Newman, propping the gun against the wall, convinced that he has entered a madhouse. Could someone please tell me what's going on and why Charlotte's locked in the bathroom?

⟨◦⟩

Still flustered, Beth leads Mr. Newman into the living room and closes the door. The walls are painted a lemon yellow and covered with framed drawings of birds all looking as if they are about to fly out through the glass.

Beth tells Mr. Newman the circumstances of Lily's disappearance, about the police effort, about Charlotte's hysteria.

I wanted to make sure she didn't do herself harm, Richard. She was out of control and was being sick and was determined to go outside in the wind and rain and darkness to search for Lily. I thought keeping her safe in the bathroom was the best solution.

Mr. Newman looks at Beth—her wet sweatpants clinging to her fat thighs, her wet blond hair falling in front of her flabby face like brandy butter dribbling down the sides of a Christmas pudding—and comments dryly, I think it's safe to let her out now.

They walk up the stairs in silence. Beth fumbles around in her pocket for the key, pulls it out, and nervously opens the bathroom door. Charlotte's bloodshot, watery green eyes flash at her like bleeding emeralds. Charlotte spits in her face. Mr. Newman grabs his wife and pulls her into an embrace before she can do anything else.

I'll make us all some vegetable soup and garlic bread, Beth says, feeling hated and alienated. She hurries down the stairs.

Charlotte nuzzles into Mr. Newman's jumper, her tears gushing soundlessly into the tobacco-smelling woolen fibers. Mr. Newman kisses the top of her head, feeling as if he is holding a child rather than a wife, and feels even more guilty than he did before.

Joseph and Nest come out at the other end of the forest and sit down together, arm in arm, on a fallen tree trunk. The rain has stopped. They look out at a melon-slice moon in a star-sprinkled indigo sky.

I'll never be able to make love to you in the forest again, Nest whispers. The thought of some slimy Mushroom Man skulking about freaks me out.

It was only a fairy tale, Joseph replies sadly.

But it looks as though there's some horrible truth in that fairy tale, Nest insists, snuggling up closer to him.

We can't say anything for sure yet.

They both look out at the dark fields flooding into the horizon, the windows of the vicarage still blazing like a lighthouse.

I think Mr. Jones fancies your mum, Nest says matter-of-factly. Joseph looks repulsed. And I think it would do them both good to get together.

Mum would never be interested, Joseph answers dismissively.

I'm not so sure, persists Nest. She always hums whilst she's doing the cooking whenever he's about to come around for Sunday lunch, and she always gives him a large slice of her homemade ginger cake to take home. And she's lonely and she often looks sad even though she tries her very best not to.

So? Joseph is irritated.

So I don't know why she wouldn't want to get together with him.

the mushroom man

◦

Jacob Jones wears his solitude like the lumpy mole on his neck he's never gotten around to getting cut off. Every day he acknowledges it in the mirror when he is shaving, considers making an appointment at the doctor's surgery, and is put off by the thought of the half-hour drive to town and the disruption to his daily routine. Jacob Jones sticks by his daily routine the same way he sticks by the members of his parish community. And he's content. He really has found peace with the Lord, and he finds pleasure in devoting his life to his faith, and in a chocolate chip brownie or a slice of Beth's ginger cake with a nice cup of tea, followed by a nice suck on his pipe, every afternoon at four o'clock.

Jacob Jones also finds pleasure in secretly writing his own poetry. In the evenings after dinner, he likes to sit at his desk in his candlelit attic, with his pipe and a plate of apple slices, raisins, and dried apricots, and scribble all kinds of ponderings in the notebook with clouds on the front cover, which he bought especially for this poem-composing purpose.

That night Jacob Jones is sitting at his attic desk, nibbling on a dried apricot and reading Dylan Thomas by candlelight for inspiration. During this private part of the day, Jacob Jones allows himself to think about Beth and her warm face and kind eyes. He fits her into graceful similes in his poems, and in metaphorical moments camouflages her as unique wildlife species. Then he slips the notebook under the carpet, blows out the candles, and climbs downstairs to brush his teeth, say his final prayers, and go to bed.

☙

Mr. Newman isn't tempted by the lumpy pea-green soup Beth is copiously ladling out or the charred garlic baguette placed on a stainless-steel serving dish in the middle of the table like some gone-wrong pièce de résistance. He takes a flashlight and a map, and candidly informing Charlotte that she is in no fit state to go outside searching with him, that she would be more burdensome than helpful, that they didn't need any more casualties at this stage, he walks purposefully out the door into a foreign landscape with the confidence and ignorance of a Boy Scout on his first hiking trip.

Charlotte scoops up some soup with her spoon and lets it trickle back into the bowl. Scoop, trickle. Scoop, trickle. Scoop, trickle. As if she is screening it for some clue as to what she has done to deserve ending up in such a dire state of affairs.

Charlotte, pet, please try and eat something, pleads Beth.

Charlotte ignores her. Scoop, trickle. Scoop, trickle.

I'm sorry for locking you in the bathroom. I was just so worried you would go outside and make yourself even more unwell.

I hate you, Charlotte says, without looking up from her soup. I came to visit you to give you a second chance, and you just make a mockery of it.

Beth tries to hold back her tears, stuffing down garlic bread even though she doesn't have the appetite.

I don't know what Mother and Father will say when they hear what you have done, continues Charlotte.

I've only done what I thought best, replies Beth, her voice wobbling.

Best for whom? Charlotte counters. Best for an abductor? You allowed your children to lose Lily not only once but twice and thereby gave an abductor the opportunity to thoroughly ensnare her. You allowed your children to tell Lily a fairy tale, so that she believed this abductor was a nice fairy person. And you directly helped this abductor by hampering my chances of searching, by locking me up like an animal in the bathroom. Charlotte pushes away her soup. It looks vile.

Beth stands, shaking convulsively. She moves around the table to Charlotte, picks up the bowl of untouched soup, pours it over her head, puts the bowl down, and walks out of the kitchen, ignoring her sister's shrieking.

~♂○

Beth lumbers up the stairs to check on the triplets, whom she earlier sent to bed. She prays they did not overhear their aunt's accusations.

Apparently they didn't. The three girls are each snuggled up under their multicolored blankets with the lights off, talking about searching techniques for an invisible fairy Lily.

How are you feeling, Amy, angel? Beth walks over and sits on the edge of her bed.

Much better, thank you, Mummy, Amy answers.

Good. Beth strokes her cheek and kisses her forehead. Sleep tight, my darling.

Good night, Mummy. Amy kisses her back.

Beth goes to Jude and Sam and kisses each of them on the forehead also, before walking out of the room, closing the door softly behind her.

10

Mr. Newman strides down the slope in Wellingtons that have tasted only urban juices, and clears his throat several times to announce himself to a countryside sprawling out in still, silent sleep.

Mr. Newman is convinced that he will find Lily. He half expects to find her sitting at the bottom of the slope—dangling her red Wellies into the stream and chatting away to Eeyore from *Winnie-the-Pooh*, just waiting for Daddy to scoop her up onto his shoulders and carry her back to the house. Mr. Newman doesn't believe that really bad things can affect his relatively rosy life. Mr. Newman doesn't believe that it won't be "and they lived happily ever after." Mr. Newman truly believes that he will find Lily when no one else has, that it's just a question of looking harder.

Mr. Newman also believes that his finding Lily will be a gesture of marital resurrection, that it will show that he is able to salvage something from the mess they have gotten themselves into. He can see it like a scene from a movie: Himself as an Indiana Jones walking up the slope with a laughing Lily on his shoulders, Charlotte running down in a long see-through white dress, arms open wide, to greet them.

Mr. Newman gets to the stream, waves his flashlight around, and splashes across to the forest.

Charlotte has locked herself in her bedroom. She takes off the soup-soiled sweater and pants, and stuffs them out of sight under the wardrobe. She opens the bottom drawer of the chest and rummages to make sure that the lilac paper with the round sticker saying "With Best Wishes from the Little Welsh Bobbin Lace Shop" really has been removed. She checks the other drawers.

She pulls off the lace thong she is wearing and places it flat on the floor. She takes the nail scissors from her toiletry bag and sits down cross-legged and bare-bottomed, and methodically cuts up the thong. She cuts into two, into four, into six, into eight . . . until all that is left resembles a pile of snowflakes. She sweeps these up with her hands and drops them into the dustbin.

It is then that she sees Lily's drawing of the Mushroom Man with the red streak across it. A piercing pang, a surging in her chest, and tears that try in vain to cry out her pain.

She pulls the drawing out carefully to examine it.

⋞◯

Mr. Newman hears a muffled sound of footsteps advancing toward him. He feels a chill, the hard, fast pumping of his heart, and a sudden sense of his lack of preparation. He switches off his flashlight and crouches behind a tree. He sees a yellow gleam. Two simultaneous yellow gleams. The sound of footsteps is coming from two separate directions.

Stop! A male voice.

Mr. Newman nearly jumps out of his skin. Me? He wonders. Surely I haven't been seen.

The footsteps stop. An illuminated, bodiless female face appears out of the darkness a little distance away.

I love you, the male voice says.

I love you too, replies the female head. But your light is hurting my eyes.

⋞◯

Beth lingers in the kitchen, mopping the floor sticky with soup and speckled with cheese and cream cracker crumbs, and looking for other dirt to wash away. She is listening to country-western music on the radio because her husband always used to listen to country-western music when he was working, and it reminds her of walking into the shed with a cup of tea and a slice of almond cake and him looking up and smiling at her.

Beth ponders about why she and her husband loved each other so much. They loved each other with the wonder and passion of teenagers falling in love for the first time, every day that they were together. When they were in their forties he stroked and kissed her breasts with the same devoted gentleness and awe as when she first allowed him to touch her, in a field run over with bluebells in the middle of nowhere, when they were nineteen. He still wrote her silly love messages with a drawing of a strawberry in the corner — they had met on a strawberry-picking holiday in Norway — and brought her lemon sherbet every week that they were married, just as he had when they were dating. They never stopped nighttime skinny-dipping in the river, sloshing back whiskey from a bottle while their bodies were numbed by ice-cold water. It was as if they had never aged.

Maybe that was the reason, Beth concludes. Maybe the reason we loved each other so much was that we always behaved like kids on a permanent adventure.

Who are you? booms a voice from the darkness of the forest.

Joseph and Nest scream and run toward each other. Do you think it's the Mushroom Man? whispers Nest, petrified.

And what are you doing wandering around in the middle of the forest in the early hours of the morning? persists the voice.

Joseph collects himself and points his flashlight in the direction of the booming voice. My name's Joseph Griffiths, he answers, trying to sound confident. His flashlight beam rests on a vaguely familiar face. Uncle Richard?

⁓✺◯

Amy cannot sleep. Her head aches and she is worried sick about Lily. She sits up in bed and looks out the window at the stars twinkling like diamonds and the banana moon dangling above the forest. She thinks she can see a female face in the night sky, smiling and winking sideways at her: her sunny smile is the banana moon, and her winking eyes are the brightest diamond stars.

Princess Fairymostbeautiful! gasps Amy.

Amy is sure she can see Princess Fairymostbeautiful's eyes glisten extra-bright in acknowledgment. She kneels below the windowsill and cups her hands.

Princess Fairymostbeautiful, whispers Amy. Diamond-eyed, golden-lipped Lady of the Forest, we're all very upset. I don't think the Mushroom Man realizes the pain he's caused other people by turning Lily into an invisible fairy. Please can you have a word with him and ask him to turn Lily back into a visible human? Or maybe you can use your own powers to uninvisible and unfairy Lily?

Amy stares hard at Princess Fairymostbeautiful's celestial face for a response but can gather nothing.

Clap your hands and say that you believe in fairies, says Jude from behind her; she has been watching and listening to Amy all along. Lily reminded me of how in *Peter Pan* every time someone says the opposite of "I believe in fairies," a fairy dies, and I reread *Peter*

Pan this afternoon and there's this part about how the children make the sick fairy Tinkerbell well by clapping their hands to show that they believe in fairies.

I don't see what that's got to do with asking Princess Fairymostbeautiful to bring Lily back to us. Amy sighs.

It will make Princess Fairymostbeautiful and all the other fairies like us, replies Jude. And if they like us, they're more likely to do what we ask of them.

I believe in fairies, Amy and Jude repeat over and over together, clapping their hands. I believe in fairies.

Sam, who has also been watching and listening from her bed, joins in. I believe in fairies. I believe in fairies.

And they are sure they see Princess Fairymostbeautiful's smile glow extra-golden with pleasure.

Having joined forces, Joseph, Nest, and Mr. Newman search together until five in the morning, when they are so exhausted that trees seem to be metamorphosing into giant, punkhead people and Nest maintains that a large fallen branch a short distance away is a crocodile.

They plod up the slope toward the house. Mr. Newman plods ahead of Joseph and Nest, feeling as if he is on a bad, long-drawn-out adventure ride at a theme park: he is waiting to come out at the other end into the light, to the reality of Lily's saying she needs to go for a pee or asking for mint–chocolate chip ice cream. He cannot believe that this is really happening. He cannot believe that he is trudging about in the middle of nowhere in Wales at this hour, when he would normally be cozy in bed, dreaming of golf courses, before setting out a little later for his company's marble-floored flagship office in Canary Wharf, stopping along the way at Starbucks for a double espresso and a blueberry muffin and a goggle at the foxy cashier with juicy jet-black breasts, which always peek pertly out of her low-cut tops. He cannot believe that something horrid might have happened to his little princess.

Joseph and Nest are holding each other's hands. Joseph is in awe of Mr. Newman—his hugely self-confident air, his posh accent, his wise-looking moustache, his gold Rolex watch. Nest dislikes everything about him—the way he stares at her breasts, the way he patronizes Joseph, his pretentious moustache. Nest thinks that he is just the sort of man she would have expected Charlotte to have married.

⁂

Joseph, Nest, and Mr. Newman clang into the house. Beth, who has fallen asleep in a chair in the kitchen with her head resting on her arms on the table, leaps up to see whether they have come back with Lily.

Glum faces greet her. Her heart falls. She strokes them all on the back as they enter the corridor.

Come and have a nice mug of hot chocolate before you catch some sleep, she says. It will make you feel better.

I think I'll pass, Mr. Newman replies frostily. I'm going upstairs to check on Charlotte. Good night. He nods in Beth's direction.

Overwhelmed with compassion, Beth steps forward and embraces him. Mr. Newman finds himself hugging Beth back. He feels a clog in his throat.

God bless, Beth whispers, releasing him. Mr. Newman turns toward the stairs.

I'd love some hot chocolate. Joseph tries to sound jolly.

So would I, says Nest.

Beth smiles at them both sadly. She draws them into her arms and kisses them on the top of the head, her eyes welling with tears. You're wonderful children, she blubbers. You know that?

〇〜

Charlotte glances up with half-hopeful eyes at Mr. Newman as he enters the bedroom. He shakes his head. Charlotte drops her head into her pillow and carries on sobbing.

What time are the policemen coming back in the morning? asks Mr. Newman. He sits on the bed beside her and strokes her damp hair away from her damp face.

They said first thing.

Mr. Newman looks at his watch, then out the window at dawn emerging in uncertain grayness, then back down at Charlotte. It will be okay, he says. I know it will be okay.

You don't know, sobs Charlotte. You can't know.

I love you, whispers Mr. Newman, pressing his lips against her forehead.

You haven't loved me in a long time, Charlotte answers, pushing him away. So don't bother to start again now.

⤶◯

Joseph and Nest are snuggled up naked in bed together. Joseph starts to stroke Nest's breasts gently.

I don't want to have sex tonight, she whispers.

That's okay, Joseph whispers back, and kisses her softly on the lips.

Do you love me? Nest asks.

You're my world, answers Joseph.

A helicopter gurgling below curdled-milk clouds is the harbinger of full morning. Four police vans—sirens screeching, blue lights spinning—bump and bang up the path, lunging into the womb of the yard. Policemen and sniffer dogs spill out of the vans and into the fields with the purpose of mice teased out of their hiding holes by the sharp smell of cheese.

Except for Police Officer Number One and Police Officer Number Two. Police Officer Number One slowly slips himself down from his driver's seat, reaches for his briefcase, slams the van door, and waddles toward the house. Police Officer Number Two follows him.

Police Officer Number One raps at the door.

11

Beth, Charlotte, Mr. Newman, Police Officer Number One, and Police Officer Number Two sit around the kitchen table. Charlotte refuses to allow either Beth or Mr. Newman to rest their hands on hers as a source of comfort.

I found this. Charlotte hands Lily's drawing of the Mushroom Man with the red streak across it to Police Officer Number One.

Is this meant to be the Mushroom Man? inquires Police Officer Number One gravely. He points to the gray-bearded man in red bobble hat and cloak, with perfect pink circles for cheeks.

Yes. I asked the triplets about it.

Police Officer Number One opens his briefcase, takes out an envelope, slides the picture carefully inside, and puts the envelope back in the briefcase. I'd like you to show us the clothes Lily was wearing the two previous times she went missing, so that we can send them away for DNA testing, Police Officer Number One requests. And then I hope you don't mind if we have a quick look around the house, in Lily's bedroom in particular.

The clothes that are missing now are the clothes she wore yesterday when she went missing, answers Charlotte.

Are you sure she didn't even change her underwear? Police Officer Number Two probes cautiously.

Charlotte breaks down into tears. Mr. Newman feels red-hot-iron wrath. Beth is quivering.

⟳

Pavlova usually loves having the house to herself, because she can pretend it is her own. She can pretend she is the lady of a large (but not vulgarly large) parquet-wooden-floored Edwardian house, which has frescoes of pudgy cupids on the corridor ceilings, in the *in* part of Notting Hill Gate. She can potter around rearranging the already rearranged dried-flower collections standing stiffly in hand-painted china vases. She can try on one of Charlotte's lace-rimmed hats and her peach summer jacket and pose in front of the full mirror in the master bedroom, pouting and making silly gestures with her hands and wrists. And—her favorite—she can sit sloppily in the drawing room, using Charlotte's electric foot massager, giggling at "Etiquette for Today" in *Good Housekeeping*, and slurping mint tea with three spoonfuls of honey from a china cup.

But today Pavlova doesn't even feel like treating herself to some of the schmaltz herring and sun-dried-tomato bread that Mr. Newman bought a couple of days ago in the Harrods food department. Today Pavlova doesn't even feel like pouring herself some of Charlotte's freshly squeezed organic pink grapefruit juice in a crystal glass and adding two perfect cubes of ice. Today Pavlova just wants to make herself some plain oatmeal porridge and a mug of hot milk with a spoonful of sugar like her mum used to make for her every morning when she was younger.

When she can't find any oatmeal in the pantry, she makes herself a slice of whole-wheat toast with butter.

The triplets have not slept. Sam came up with the plan that, when it was properly light, they should go down to the forest—nearer to the fairies, where they would be able to hear better—and make it quite clear that they are believers. So as soon as all the others had finally retreated into their bedrooms, they sneaked down into the kitchen and collected three empty cylindrical ice cream cartons and three sheets of waxed paper. They spent the half-hour before dawn making drums on Amy's bed: they placed the waxed paper over the top of the ice cream cartons and fixed it tightly in place with ponytail bands. Then they decorated the cartons with the gold-glitter pens they use only for special occasions and, with pencils as drumsticks, quietly tried out their instruments.

They were very pleased with the results, until they heard the helicopter.

At least the fairies should be impressed by our effort, says Jude, trying to sound reassuring, as they dress to go down to the forest.

They better be, says Sam, whose pen has run out of gold glitter because of her enthusiastic decorating.

Amy stares out the window at the swarms of important-looking policemen with their dogs crawling around the fields, and suddenly bursts out laughing.

Charlotte and Mr. Newman are hovering upstairs in the corridor while Charlotte and Lily's bedroom is being searched. Police Officer Number One beckons them to his side at the doorway. Seeing the dustbin he is holding, Charlotte knows what is coming, and wants to melt into the ground like a snowman.

Do you know anything about these cut-up white pieces? Police Officer Number One quizzes.

Charlotte feels hot and nauseated. Yes, she mutters. I did it.

Police Officer Number One raises his eyebrows, as if he would like to hear more about this.

Mr. Newman comes to the rescue. Did what, darling? He looks puzzled.

I cut up an item of my own clothing I didn't like, Charlotte answers, desperate to haste away this moment.

Ah, says Police Officer Number One, turning back into the bedroom even more curious than before.

Why? persists Mr. Newman, quietly.

Police Officer Number One's ears prick up.

What item of clothing was it?

Police Officer Number One strains his ears from within the bedroom to gather the answer.

It's none of your business, snaps Charlotte, rushing to the bathroom to throw up again.

Police Officer Number One emerges from the bedroom, strokes his chin and addresses Mr. Newman. What kind of relationship does Lily have with her mother?

◦◦◦

Beth is gazing out the kitchen window at the men and dogs nosing around suspiciously on the slope. She takes sips of a hot lemon-honey-and-cinnamon drink, which she usually has only when she is ill, and thinks about whether there are enough ingredients for making ginger snaps for all the policemen.

The triplets walk in with their drums.

What are those for, pets? Beth stares with curiosity at the gold-glitter objects.

Drums, they announce in unison.

Drums! Beth is distressed. My sugarplums, this is no time for drums.

The triplets exchange conspiratorial looks.

Amy takes a deep breath. Mummy, we're convinced that Lily has been turned into an invisible fairy. We want to show the fairies we believe in them, to persuade them to bring Lily back to us.

Dear me! sighs Beth. She doesn't know what to say, and she wants to cry. Sit down, girls, and we'll discuss this over breakfast.

—

The triplets are taking their seats and Beth is setting the table when Police Officer Number One, Police Officer Number Two, and another police officer appear in the doorway with grave faces.

Mrs. Griffiths, may we have a word with you alone? Police Officer Number One requests.

Beth scuttles out of the kitchen, leads the policemen into the living room, and closes the door.

My colleague found these in the grass at the bottom of the slope, says Police Officer Number One, opening a brown paper bag to reveal two used condoms.

Beth gasps and her stomach churns.

We've already asked Mr. and Mrs. Newman, and they say they don't know anything about them, says Police Officer Number Two. Could you tell us anything?

Beth puts her hand to her mouth and shakes her head. I don't think so, she replies.

Police Officer Number One straightens his back.

Unless . . . Beth considers aloud. Have you shown them to my son and his girlfriend?

☙

Police Officer Number One thumps on Joseph's bedroom door.

Joseph and Nest groan. Who is it? asks Joseph.

The police, answers Police Officer Number One. Joseph and Nest scramble around for their pajamas. Can we come in?

Hang on a sec, says Joseph, his heart nearly hurting it is pumping so hard. Nest is fumbling with her pajama-top buttons.

As soon as they are both decent, Joseph opens the door.

Police Officer Number One looks Joseph and Nest in their matching blue-on-white-spotted pajamas up and down and clears his throat.

Can you tell us anything about these? he asks, opening the brown paper bag. We found them in the grass covered with a dusting of earth at the bottom of the slope.

Joseph's and Nest's ears blaze ripe-tomato red.

⌀

Jacob Jones is preparing for a ten-o'clock funeral service. An ex-headmistress of the local comprehensive, Betty Davis, who wore a mint-green suit with a matching mint-green hat and matching mint-green shoes with matching mint-green low heels, to every Sunday service for as long as he can remember, died at the age of eighty-one. It should be an occasion for celebration, Jacob Jones tries to remind himself. Betty died leaving three children, eight grandchildren, a gaggle of adoring, gossipy girlfriends, and two lovers whom she played off each other with the candid coquettishness of a seventeen-year-old, and is now soaring up to heaven to be with her husband, who died three years ago and with whom her true heart had been all along. If lives were described in terms of boxes of chocolates, Betty's would definitely be a triple-layered box of dark liqueur-filled Belgian chocolates.

But today Jacob Jones isn't in the mood to dwell on death, even if, as on this occasion, it makes the happiest of endings. Today Jacob Jones doesn't want to stand in the graveyard, staring down into a dark pit at an anonymous-looking black coffin that could be containing anyone, and lead the sermon as people drop earth on the coffin, reciting, "Earth to earth, ashes to ashes, dust to dust. The Lord bless her and keep her, the Lord make his face to shine upon her and be gracious unto her and give her peace. Amen."

12

Keep the children inside the house, Police Officer Number One orders Beth. He sits at the head of the kitchen table and scoffs down the slice of rhubarb turnover cake that Beth has warmed up for him.

The triplets, who have placed their beautifully decorated drums in a neat row at the end of the table, crunch on their Coco Pops and look up at him with desperately disappointed eyes.

Police Officer Number One ignores them. He continues addressing Beth. I don't want them getting in the way of the search. He lowers his voice. Or disappearing too.

Of course, says Beth.

Police Officer Number One finishes off his rhubarb turnover cake, wipes his mouth with a paper napkin, and stands. His chair screeches as he pushes it back. That was very tasty, Mrs. Griffiths.

Can I get you anything else?

I'm all right, thank you very much. I'd best be seeing whether Mrs. Newman's in a fit state to have a quick word alone with me now.

I'll take you up.

❦

After eating her toast, Pavlova decides to distract herself from her melancholy thoughts by snooping through the desk drawers in Charlotte's study. Pavlova has never had the opportunity to snoop in the room before: Charlotte is nearly always in it—sorting bills, writing the odd classical music concert review, writing complaints and invitations—and on the occasions when she isn't, she always locks the door. But this time, Charlotte has forgotten to lock the door. This time, the door is a tantalizing half-centimeter ajar. This time, Charlotte's study is all Pavlova's.

Pavlova smirks. She finds a Cadbury's Roses tin pushed to the back of the bottom drawer of Charlotte's desk. Pavlova pulls it out and opens it to see if there are any of her favorite sickly-sweet orange-cream chocolates left.

But the tin does not contain chocolates. It contains photo booth pictures of Mr. Newman and Charlotte when they were younger, kissing and laughing: Charlotte has a yellow rose behind her ear and Mr. Newman has a bad sixties mullet. And on the reverse, in Mr. Newman's handwriting, is written "I am forever yours xxxxxxxx."

Pavlova quickly stuffs the photos in the Cadbury's Roses tin, shoves the tin in the bottom drawer, and hurries out of the study, slamming the door behind her. She wants to go home to see her mother.

*

We are considering the possibility that Lily may have run away, says Police Officer Number One, sunken into the soft sofa in the living room opposite Charlotte.

Lily has not run away, Charlotte asserts.

Police Officer Number One scratches his scalp. It is important to try to keep an open mind, Mrs. Newman.

Charlotte scowls. I know my daughter. And I know that she would not have run away.

You can't recall a little squabble the day before she disappeared? A little disagreement, however trivial?

Charlotte shakes her head impatiently.

So she went to sleep happy?

Charlotte nods.

Your last words to each other were amicable?

Charlotte shuffles in her chair.

What were your last words?

Charlotte hesitates. I did mention we might be going home the next day, and she did seem a little disappointed.

Police Officer Number One raises his eyebrow.

But she didn't cry or anything.

Police Officer Number One scratches his nose and writes this all down on his notepad.

Even if she did run away, Charlotte bursts out, whimpering, why hasn't somebody found her by now?

❧

As soon as the triplets have finished their Coco Pops, they rush upstairs to their bedroom and close the door.

Now what? huffs Jude.

We have to escape secretly, answers Amy.

The policemen will just send us straight back when they see us, says Jude.

All three slump on their beds and look at the paint peeling off the damp ceiling for a solution.

We need to enter the forest from the other side, where there will be less policemen, says Sam.

Easier said than done, sighs Jude.

I'm sure the fairies will help us, Amy replies.

And we need more of us, says Sam. We need more children to chant "We believe in fairies" with us.

It will please the fairies more, agrees Amy. And the more the fairies are pleased, the greater the chance of getting Lily back.

How are we going to do that? asks Jude.

We're going down to the village, Sam replies. And we're going to get as many children as we can to come with us.

How's Charlotte holding up? Beth asks as Mr. Newman enters the kitchen and plops himself in the chair at the head of the table.

She's gone back into the bathroom, he answers quietly, looking at the clean tiled floor.

Beth sits in the chair beside him and rests her hand on top of his. Mr. Newman glances up at her. I don't know what I'm going to do if we don't find Lily safe and sound, he admits.

Don't think about that now, Beth urges in a soft voice.

Charlotte's not stable, says Mr. Newman. There are all these things she keeps simmering below the surface and then they all suddenly erupt at once.

But you look after her. Beth is half testing him.

Mr. Newman looks down again. It's been difficult recently, I must say.

Of course it's difficult *now*. . . .

Mr. Newman pauses. Even before now it was difficult.

Beth waits.

Mr. Newman stares at Beth's wise, round face—as comforting as the finish line at the end of a long-distance run—and wants to unburden himself of everything. I should have been more attentive, he confesses. I've been too preoccupied with my work and things lately. She deserves more.

Does she ever touch the piano? Beth asks gently. I remember she used to love playing the piano when she was younger.

Mr. Newman shakes his head. Only when she's teaching Lily. He smiles. Lily's just got the hang of one of Brahms's Hungarian Dances.

◌

The triplets twist their bedsheets into tight, fat, snakelike elongations and knot them firmly together into a single rope, one end of which Sam ties securely to the foot of Amy's bed.

Amy opens the window and takes a good look around outside. The policemen seem to be at the bottom of the slope with their backs to the house. All clear, she announces.

Jude starts to lower the rope to the ground.

Is it long enough? asks Sam.

Just about.

Is it strong enough? asks Amy.

Hope so. Jude drops the last bit of rope and stands back. There. Who wants to go down first?

◌

I can't, moans Nest. I'll die with embarrassment.

You've got to go down at some stage, Joseph reasons. Don't be silly.

I can't. I can't. They'll all stare at us. She walks to the window. Do you think it's too far to jump to the ground from here?

Are you cuckoo?

Nest opens the window, catches sight of Amy descending on the bedsheet rope, and bursts out laughing. Josie, come and look at this! Nest squeals.

Shhhhh, Amy pleads. Don't tell anyone. She gets to the bottom. Jude starts descending.

What on earth are you doing? demands Joseph.

Shhhhh, Jude and Amy repeat together. Jude gets to the bottom. Sam descends, on her back a rucksack containing their gold-glitter drums.

I'm going down that way too, announces Nest.

What? Joseph grabs her arm. Nest shakes him off and disappears out the doorway.

Joseph turns to the triplets, who are now all on the ground glimpsing up at him guiltily.

Please don't tell anyone, begs Amy.

Why don't you go outside the normal way? Joseph asks.

We're just having a bit of fun, Jude says in a wholly unconvincing voice. She catches sight of Nest at the windowsill about to climb down. And your girlfriend's also giving it a go, so it can't be such a bad idea.

The triplets scamper off.

You're cuckoo, Nest, you're totally cuckoo. Joseph, exasperated, watches her descend. And the rope's probably not strong enough for you. You'll probably fall.

But the rope is strong enough. Nest gets to the bottom, lets out a sigh of relief, and waves up at him.

You'll have to come to my place if you want to see me in the near future, she tells Joseph, laughing, before running off.

Joseph is too stunned to shout anything back.

The coffin is lowered slowly into the pit. Silence, apart from a robin redbreast twittering in a nearby elm tree and the sniffling of friends and relatives mourning their own mortality.

Jacob Jones swallows hard and begins the final prayers.

13

Beth runs through her fields, darting from one policeman to another, asking whether they have seen her triplets. She feels like an energetic pencil-tip doing a detailed connect-the-dots.

She finds Police Officer Number One supervising a dig in the marsh. Have you seen the triplets? she shouts to him.

Police Officer Number One walks over to her, looking blank. I thought I asked you to keep them in the house, he chides.

I tried, Beth answers meekly, but they escaped. My son said he saw them climb down to the ground from their bedroom window with a makeshift rope and then run off.

Police Officer Number One rolls his eyes. This is the last thing we need right now, he mutters impatiently.

I'm so sorry.

How long ago did they leave the house?

Two hours, and no one seems to have seen them since.

Police Officer Number One unhooks his walkie-talkie from his belt, presses the red button on the side, and speaks into it. We have a new problem, he begins.

Ow

We should only ask a child to come with us if they're not with someone older, says Sam, as they walk toward the village playground. We don't want some older person trying to stop what we're doing.

Good point, Amy agrees. Jude nods.

They open a gate painted with a rainbow into the playground. Two chestnut-haired girls with pigtails spin on the merry-go-round, a baby-faced blond boy and a dark-skinned girl ride on the seesaw, and a fat boy with glasses is about to fall from the monkey bars. In one corner, a young, bedraggled-looking woman sits on a sky-blue bench, bouncing a bawling baby on her lap. The triplets vaguely recognize the children from when they were on monitor duty last year, looking after the younger classes in the school dining hall.

The bawling gets even louder. The fat boy falls from the monkey bars.

Can't you take him home, Mam? the fat boy moans. I can't do the monkey bars when he's screaming so loud.

The young woman stands. He needs a feed anyway, she says, stroking the baby's huge, hairless head. But haven't you had enough, Dick? Don't you want to come home now?

Dick, who is already lumbering up the stepladder again, shakes his head. I want to get to the end of the monkey bars, he replies.

Very well, then, she sighs. But don't be long. She blinks twice at the triplets before letting herself out through the rainbow gate.

⌒

Pavlova picks up the telephone receiver and dials an unfamiliar number.

Hallo.

Tatiana?

Pavlova!

I'm coming back home.

Are you okay?

I'm fine. Her voice breaks against her will. I just want to come home.

That's great.

Can I stay with you?

A short pause. Sure. Her voice is slightly strained.

Just temporarily, of course, until I find my own place.

It will be good to catch up.

I could stay with Mum like I normally do, but I know you've finished that spare room now. . . .

We've put a lovely brown and purple carpet in it, Tatiana says proudly.

My flight arrives tomorrow night at ten.

I'll meet you at the airport.

Sam and Jude roll their gold-glitter drums to get everybody's attention.

The merry-go-round stops spinning, the dark-skinned girl is left wiggling her legs in midair, and Dick falls from the monkey bars again.

Cowpats! he groans. I was nearly at the end.

Ladies and gentlemen, Amy begins, holding forth from the top of the slide, we need your help. Our six-year-old cousin Lily has gone missing. We think she has been turned into an invisible fairy by someone called the Mushroom Man. The only way we can get her back is to get as many children as possible to march into the forest bordering our farm shouting "We believe in fairies." We think this will make the fairies like us and want to help us. Amy holds her hands out toward her audience theatrically. Please come with us — a little girl's life is in danger. You can save a little girl's life.

The two chestnut-haired girls, recognizing the triplets as the monitors who didn't force them to eat their chili con carne, bounce down from the merry-go-round, pigtails swinging. We'll help, one of them offers.

So will I, shouts the dark-skinned girl, saluting the triplets from above the ground.

Me too, yells the baby-faced blond boy, who stands abruptly from the seesaw, making the dark-skinned girl drop to the ground with a big bump.

Ouch! she squeaks.

The baby-faced boy apologizes profusely, the *r*'s in "sorry" lisping out as sad little *w*'s, and rushes over to help her up.

The triplets turn to Dick, who is persevering his way up the stepladder yet again. I don't believe in that stupid girlie fairy stuff, he informs them.

Amy scowls at him. Well, that's why you can never get to the end of the monkey bars.

I can get to the end of the monkey bars, Dick spits back.

Can't, replies Amy.

Can.

Show us, then.

Dick braves the monkey bars again. Three bars from the end, he falls off again.

See, says Amy.

I was so nearly there, he mumbles moodily.

But so nearly there's still not the end.

Dick sticks his tongue out at her. Amy ignores it.

I promise, if you come with us now, you will be able to reach the end of the monkey bars the next time you try, she tells him.

❧

Having been ordered to remain in the house, Beth paces around the kitchen. She fidgets frantically and, as if keeping time with the loud tick of the sunshine-faced clock, snatches looks out the window at the front garden path.

Charlotte and Mr. Newman enter the kitchen. Charlotte is clutching one of Lily's dresses—a blue-and-white-striped sailor style with a big lace-rimmed collar—and Mr. Newman has taken off his gold Rolex.

No news of the triplets either? asks Mr. Newman, guiding Charlotte to a chair.

Beth shakes her head. I can't believe it. I can't believe they've just disappeared like that.

Charlotte sneaks a peek at Beth's face, decides that she has been crying, and then retreats into wallowing in her own misery.

Sit down, Mr. Newman tells Beth gently. I'll make us all a cup of tea.

I'd rather stand, she answers nervously, stepping from one foot to the other. But a cup of tea would be great.

Mr. Newman turns to Charlotte. Would you like a cup of tea, darling?

Charlotte shakes her head.

It will do you good, you know, Beth says. If you're not eating, you should at least have something to drink.

Charlotte sniffles. Okay, then, she whispers.

Mr. Newman rolls up his sleeves and fills the kettle.

⁂

Jacob Jones is at Betty Davis's funeral reception, in what was her favorite teashop in the village. Betty came here every Friday afternoon with her gaggle of gaga girlfriends and ordered Welsh teacakes with clotted cream and gooseberry jam and extra-large Irish coffees. You could see them all through the window with their blue-rinse hairdos and shocking-pink lips, cackling like geese and dragging away compulsively at their Silk Cut cigarettes as if they contained stealthy, virile extra seconds they could stick on at the end of their ever-shrinking allotted span.

Jacob Jones is disappointed. The reception is a dismal affair, with the soft, soporific hum of hushed, solemn talk, lukewarm Earl Grey tea, and overcooked cheese scones. A disloyal tribute to such an effervescent sunburst of a character.

He feels a prod in his back as he puts his plate with its half-eaten scone on a table. He turns around. Two of Betty's girlfriends grin at him from under their huge flying-saucer hats.

When are you and Beth Griffiths going to get it properly together, then? asks the one with electrifyingly radiant rouged cheeks.

Pardon? Jacob Jones knocks back a huge gulp of cold tea.

It's been a good two years now since he died, the other one says, taking out a cigarette. A bit of nooky's perfectly acceptable now.

The two old ladies chortle like pigs.

Jacob Jones turns away.

⁂

Where d'you think you're going, young man? Beth demands, as she sees Joseph heading for the door.

To Nest's.

I'm not letting you go wandering off and disappearing too.

Mum, I'm sixteen years old, I'm five-foot-nine, and I'm a brown belt in judo.

Beth takes a deep breath. You never know, Joseph. I don't want to take any risks.

This is ridiculous, he huffs, and storms upstairs and toward the triplets' room.

He stands in their doorway and looks in: their gold-glitter pens are lying on the floor and their makeshift rope is still dangling from the window like a long lizard's tongue.

He suddenly feels a hand on his shoulder. He jumps and turns around. His mother is staring at him despairingly, with watery eyes.

Joseph, do you have any idea how serious this situation is? she says, her voice trembling.

14

We still need a few more of us, says Sam. How about we go to the sweetshop? There are always children there.

Everyone—especially Dick, who has decided to come after all, and whose mother recently banned him from buying any more Everlasting Gobstoppers—shows enthusiasm for the idea. The triplets hurry everybody along to the corner sweetshop, where the woman at the counter has a set of false teeth that falls out whenever she talks too much.

Once inside the lair of mouthwatering, teeth-rotting treats, Dick heads straight for the Everlasting Gobstoppers, the chestnut-haired girls for the cherry Lipstick Lollipops, the dark-skinned girl for the Popping Candy, and the blond baby-faced boy for the wild cherry Hubba Bubba bubble gum. Jude and Sam are eyeing the Sherbet Dip Dabs, but Amy takes them aside.

There are three unaccompanied children here, Amy whispers. One for each of us. Sam, you go and talk to that boy with the green spiky hair. Jude, you take the girl with the pink headband. I'll go for the girl with the scabs on her knees—I think I once gave her one of my favorite furry stickers from my sticker album.

The triplets creep up like cuddly bears to their prey, and wait for the right moment to pounce.

⌒∽

There is a slow and solemn knocking from below.

Beth rushes down the stairs, nearly slipping she is moving so fast, and opens the door.

Police Officer Number One is standing with two other policemen beside him and is avoiding her eyes.

Beth is bursting.

We haven't found the triplets or Lily yet, says Police Officer Number One. But we have found a couple of things we would like you to identify.

What? Beth chokes, feeling as if someone is rubbing a sharp icicle against the raw bone of her spine.

Police Officer Number One clears his throat. I think it's best if we disclose any information to all of you together. Could you take us to Mr. and Mrs. Newman, please?

Beth leads the men into the kitchen, where Charlotte is clutching her mug of tea with both hands and Mr. Newman is stirring some oatmeal in a saucepan over the stove. They look up fearfully at the three police officers, who take off their hats and stand in a straight line with expressionless faces, the shiny silver buttons on their uniforms catching the midday sun.

Police Officer Number One pulls on transparent plastic gloves and takes out two small red Wellingtons and a pair of polka-dotted socks from a plastic bag. Charlotte wails and drops her mug on the floor. Beth and Mr. Newman rush to her side.

I take it you think these are Lily's, then, says Police Officer Number One. Could you have a closer look to make sure?

The polka-dotted socks are definitely Lily's, Charlotte whimpers. If the Wellingtons are a children's size eight and have frog-print soles, then they are hers also.

Police Officer Number One turns the boots upside down and examines the soles. They are a children's size eight and they have frog-print soles.

Charlotte's arms shake.

Where did you find them? asks Mr. Newman, as bright white lights start to fizz and spit across his vision like fireworks.

In the middle of the forest, replies Police Officer Number One.

⚬

The two girls in the sweetshop are easily recruited, but not the boy with the green spiky hair. Fuck off, he shouts in Sam's face, and then helps himself to some Liquorice Spiders. I don't give a shit about stupid Mushroom Men or fairies, and I'll bust your guts if you don't get your fat face out of my way.

The woman with the false teeth comes out from behind the counter and tells the boy to leave. I won't have any children who use foul language like that in my shop, she says crossly.

I'm just gonna buy my Liquorice Spiders and then I'll be gone for good, the boy replies.

You're not buying any of my nice Liquorice Spiders after nasty language like that.

Please.

Out! Now! And I don't want to see you in here again before you've picked up some manners! Her teeth are on the verge of falling out. She pushes them back in.

The boy leaves his Pick-'n'-Mix bag on the counter and sulkily drags his feet out of the shop.

Amy turns to the woman. How much would you charge me for the rest of the jar of Liquorice Spiders?

The woman is taken aback. All the rest of the jar?

Amy nods.

The woman contemplates the three-quarters-full jar of long, thin black legs. Five pounds, she says.

The deal's done, then, Amy declares.

There's one more thing, says Police Officer Number One. We found nine fruit stones by the socks and Wellingtons.

He pulls on a new pair of transparent plastic gloves and reaches into another plastic bag. He takes out a handful of stones. Can you identify the fruit these stones may have come from and explain why they were there?

Beth, Charlotte, and Mr. Newman gather around his hand.

They're plum stones, Beth asserts. I can say so for definite because we have a couple of plum trees by our stream and we eat the fruit from them at this time of year.

Charlotte, pale and horrified, grips the chair behind her. The picture Lily drew of the Mushroom Man . . . , she stammers. There were plums on the table beside the Mushroom Man in the picture Lily drew.

Police Officer Number One raises an eyebrow. If that is so, Mrs. Newman, then it is of great consequence indeed. I have the picture right here. Let's take a look.

⌒

Amy rushes out to the street with the Liquorice Spiders in a brown paper bag and runs up to the boy with the green spiky hair, who is sitting on a bench, moodily lighting matches, watching the flame lick to the end of each, and then blowing the flame out just as it is about to burn his finger.

I thought I just told you to fuck off, fat face, says the boy.

Not me, Amy replies. You were talking to my triplet sister.

Yeh, right. The boy laughs, unconvinced.

Didn't you notice in the shop? asks Amy. She turns and points to Sam and Jude, standing with their new, fresh-faced entourage down the street. See?

The boy with the green spiky hair sees.

That's spooky shit! he exclaims.

Amy puts her hands on her hips and tries to look tough. Yeh, it's really spooky shit. We're a really spooky set of sisters.

The boy lights another match. They both watch the flame lick to the end of the stick.

Come with us, Amy urges in a quiet voice. We need a hard guy on our side to help us out with this mission.

The boy blows out the flame and looks at Amy. Mission?

The one my sister told you about —

The boy rolls his eyes. Oh, *that* one. He gets up from the bench. No, thanks.

Too spooky for you to handle?

What? Wee little fairies and a dumb Mushroom Man?

Formidable fairies and a magic-concocting Mushroom Man with invisible-making powers who has kidnapped an innocent little girl . . .

The boy contemplates Amy's emphatic black eyebrows and chews on a matchstick.

And . . . , Amy continues, now revealing the contents of the brown paper bag. The boy with the green spiky hair goggles. . . . you can have all these Liquorice Spiders at the end if you come with us.

Sure I'll come, replies the boy unhesitatingly.

Ⓞ⤴

And so there are, Police Officer Number One says gravely, examining the purple balls with tiny dashes coming out of the top in Lily's picture. This is a highly significant development.

Charlotte faints, flops to the ground like a puppet whose strings have just snapped. Her hard head goes smack on the ceramic tiles.

Beth and Mr. Newman yelp. They rush over to her and gently lift her head. There isn't any blood. The policemen don't step out of their straight, firm, blue-uniformed wall. They just stand still and stare and look unruffled, as if they see things like this all the time.

Charlotte, darling, Mr. Newman whispers in her ear. Charlotte, darling, can you hear us?

Charlotte opens her eyes and looks ahead vacantly.

I didn't buy the lace thong, she murmurs. I didn't buy the lace thong from the Little Welsh Bobbin Lace Shop in the village which was wrapped up in lilac tissue paper.

◯

Jacob Jones slowly makes his way to the door, squeezing people's limp hands warmly and nodding his head consolingly, smiling reassuringly and pronouncing his good-byes sincerely. He tries to avoid the two flying saucers near the door.

But they zoom straight at him.

Mr. Jonessss, they hiss. One more little word, please.

The one with the cherry cheeks beckons with her bony, wrinkled index finger like a witch for him to lean toward them. Jacob Jones reluctantly kinks his neck a fraction.

You're hot stuff underneath that stiff starched white collar, Mr. Jones, the other one whispers.

Jacob Jones blinks hard and steps back. They move forward.

You just need to loosen up a bit, she advises, winking at him.

I must be on my way. Jacob Jones again attempts to head for the door.

But Cherry Cheeks clutches his arm, making tut-tut-tut noises. Don't be a cowardly custard, Mr. Jones, she chides. Or at least don't be a cowardly custard with Beth. He feels a warm breath tickling his neck. Unless you want to become as sad a case as us two. She lets him go.

Jacob Jones watches Betty's friends disappear into the crowd. Finally he steps out the door into the early-afternoon sunshine and the comfort of the village shops in their neat, unchanging order.

○≫

Pavlova has let down her long blond hair and is staring at herself in the mirror. She holds a big pair of scissors.

She gathers in her hand the front strands of her hair from the left side of her head and with the scissors snips through the middle.

She gathers and snips until the bathroom floor has turned into a straw-bestrewn sheep pen and a wide-eyed young woman with a neat nondescript bob smiles sweetly back at her.

15

Goodness gracious! Jacob Jones gasps when he spies the triplets bounding down the other side of the street toward him, with a train of eight younger laughing, leaping-to-keep-up children, some of whom he recognizes as attending his Sunday-morning services with their parents.

He crosses the street to meet them. When the triplets notice him, their faces fall and they slow to a walk until they can see the cheese-scone crumbs on his jacket.

The triplets halt. Mr. Jones! they says nervously, positioning themselves in a line that blocks the narrow pavement and leaning into one another in a vain attempt to conceal their followers, most of whom, also recognizing Mr. Jones, jump up, yell out, and wave at him over the triplets' shoulders.

Mr. Jones stares at them in concerned bewilderment. Any news of your cousin yet? he asks anxiously.

The triplets shake their heads. We're off to try and get her back now, Amy says.

Get her back? Mr. Jones puzzles to himself. He catches sight of the gold-glitter drums in the triplets' hands and the sweets with which the younger children bopping up and down behind them are stuffing themselves and wonders what on earth is going on. Did your mother drive you down here? he inquires.

The triplets' faces flush poppy-flower red. We just walked, Sam says, in a ludicrously cheerful voice.

Walked! Surely your mother didn't allow you to walk all the way down here?

She did, lies Jude. She wanted us all out of the way whilst the police were searching.

Mr. Jones is perplexed. Why didn't she get in touch with me? He muses out loud, a little hurt. She knows I would be more than happy to have you stay at the vicarage.

You know Mummy doesn't like to put anyone out, replies Jude slyly.

Well, let me at least take you to my place now, says Mr. Jones.

The triplets look at one another, panicked.

We can't, we offered to look after all this lot for the afternoon, Amy stammers.

Mr. Jones is even more perplexed. I really don't like to see you all wandering around like this right now, he says. I'll help you take these children back to their homes, and then you can come back with me.

Impossible, answers Sam, thinking quickly. Their parents all went away for the afternoon, that's why they asked us to look after them.

Mr. Jones scratches his head. Then I'll have to take all of them also, he concludes. I can't stay in the village with you, since a couple who are thinking of getting married in the chapel have an appointment with me in my house in half an hour. It will be a squash, but there should be just about enough room in the Land Rover.

⚬

When the policemen have gone, Beth goes to her studio and closes the door. She collapses onto the old armchair where, during the summer she decided to paint them, she made each of her children sit for her. The chair coughs out dust with her impact.

The studio is Beth's space. The studio has always been where Beth is not a mother or a wife or a daughter or a sister. The studio is Beth's desert island in her spider-web world of inescapable and finely defined roles and responsibilities. Here Beth can temporarily make her own rules. Here Beth can dabble (with paint). Here Beth can mess up. Here Beth can be the supreme, all-powerful, all-controlling creator.

Here Beth is Beth without a maiden name or a married name. Here Beth can even pretend to be someone else.

Today, sitting in the old armchair staring at plain white walls being caressed by sun shafts slipping onto and slithering over them, Beth tries to pretend to be someone else. She closes her eyes. She imagines she is floating at that edge where sky evaporates into an endless, unfathomable universe. But all she can think about is how she should have remembered her camera to take pictures to show her children.

Mr. Newman carries Charlotte in his arms upstairs into her bedroom. Her body is light, and limp except for her arms, which are shaking. He feels as if he is carrying one of those half-dead birds which often end up beneath the French windows of their new extension. Such a change, he cannot help thinking, from when he carried her with one of his T-shirts twisted and wrapped over her eyes into their honeymoon suite overlooking the sea on Santorini, where there were cold white peaches on their bed which he rolled over her warm, flat tummy.

He lays her gently on the bed, props her head comfortably on a pillow, and holds an icepack to her swelling forehead. He holds her sweaty hand.

I love you, he whispers. And he really does mean it this time, in this moment confronted by torturous guilt and a face that is pained and wounded and that reminds him of his daughter. And he is desperate for her to say it back, however quietly, however halfheartedly. Say it! he is screaming in his head. For God's sake, just say it!

But Charlotte's eyelids do not even flutter in recognition. Her arms just keep quivering like the wings of one of those birds deceived.

⟡

Can we all go for a little walk? Amy asks, when the Land Rover stuffed with chattering children pulls in front of the vicarage.

Jacob Jones hesitates. I'd rather you all stayed inside with me so that I can keep a proper eye on everyone. This couple will be here any minute, so I wouldn't be able to come with you.

We won't go far, Amy promises. We'll stay in sight of the house.

And you don't want a house full of noisy children when that couple comes around, adds Jude.

Jacob Jones yanks the brake and turns off the engine.

Dick and the boy with the green spiky hair have started to sing an alternative version of "Ten Green Bottles Sitting on a Wall." Ten shitty bottoms sitting on a wall, they chant. Ten shitty bottoms sitting on a wall. If one shitty bottom should accidentally fall, there'll be nine shitty bottoms sitting on a wall. . . . The others join in, giggling.

All right, then, Jacob Jones answers reluctantly. But stick together and make sure you stay close to the house so that I can keep a good eye on you.

The triplets wink at one another.

⟡

Beth hears a sharp rap at the front door again, which she has come to recognize as Police Officer Number One's self-announcement.

She plummets from space with a plonk, rushes out of her studio, and opens the door.

We've had a sighting of the triplets in the village, Police Officer Number One divulges, his face more grave than ever. Standing beside him are Police Officer Number Two and another officer.

Beth looks flabbergasted. In the village?

They were seen getting into a large car with several younger-looking children.

Oh my God! She feels sick. Who told you this?

Mrs. Williams, the butcher's wife. She says she knows what the triplets look like, because they come in with you every Saturday morning. Apparently she tried to call to them, but she was too far away and the car drove off very quickly. She said she couldn't see whether it was a man or a woman who was driving.

Oh my God! Was Lily with them?

We asked Mrs. Williams if she thought she saw a six-year-old blonde girl, but she said she couldn't remember.

Although Beth is trying to control herself, she breaks down into tears.

You can't think of anyone's large car your triplets would have got into with several other children? quizzes Police Officer Number One.

Beth shakes her head.

You can't think of any reason why your triplets would have got into anyone's large car with several other children?

Beth shakes her head again. They've been kidnapped, like Lily! The words burst out, of their own accord, and she feels her whole body trembling.

Now, let's not jump to any conclusions yet, says Police Officer Number One. He guides her into the kitchen, sits her down on a chair, and orders Police Officer Number Two to get her a glass of water.

Beth feels as if someone has numbed her tongue, and the police officers' movements seem painfully slow, heavy, and labored—just the way she remembers her husband's last gestures from his hospital bed the day before he passed away. She stares at the water settling in the glass that Police Officer Number Two places in front of her, and the sun shooting through it, fracturing into all the colors of the rainbow on the table.

⤶○

The triplets, halfheartedly playing stuck-in-the-mud with the rest of the children, watch the smiling couple disembark from their shiny red Mini and walk to the front door of the vicarage, holding hands. The young woman has long, silky auburn hair tied in a girlish ponytail with a white ribbon and is wearing a knee-length flowery skirt and a raspberry-pink blouse. The young man has well-defined cheekbones and a prominent jaw and is dressed in light brown trousers and a light blue shirt, the top two buttons undone to reveal a tuft of thick, dark chest hair.

The children watch the door open, and see Jacob Jones shake the couple's hands and invite them into the house.

Stop! shouts Amy, holding both her hands up.

All the children stop. Amy calls for them to gather around her, as she repeatedly looks back at the house.

After a count of three, we're going to run down into the forest at the bottom of the field, she says quietly. And when we reach the forest, everyone has to chant "We believe in fairies" as loudly as possible.

⟡

I couldn't carry on living if Lily's dead, Charlotte murmurs.

Please don't say things like that, Mr. Newman begs, horrified.

Not only was I almost unable to have a child, but when I do eventually have a child, I can't even look after her properly.

Don't torture yourself like this, Charlotte. His voice is cracking.

What kind of woman am I? She stares at the ceiling abstractedly.

You're a wonderful, wonderful wife and mother.

But my husband's fucking someone else, she whimpers. My husband's fucking a sluttish twenty-three-year-old.

Mr. Newman feels as if a bullet has just been shot up his bum. He swallows. That's not true, he stammers.

I know, Charlotte says bitterly. Please don't insult me by trying to deceive me even further.

⟡

Police Officer Number One's walkie-talkie beeps. He unhooks it from his belt and presses down the red button.

Number One receiving . . .

Four more children have been reported missing from the village, an alarmed voice crackles from the walkie-talkie. One of those has been confirmed by Mrs. Williams as having entered the same car as the Griffiths triplets.

Beth grabs the hair close to her scalp and pulls at it hard. She looks up at the little dots made by uncontrollable rocketlike popcorn kernels on the ceiling above the stove. Oh, heaven help us, O Lord.

I'm going outside to talk to all my men, announces Police Officer Number One.

⋇⃝

We believe in fairies, chant all the children, entering deeper and deeper into the forest. The triplets roll their drums. We believe in fairies.

And from a short distance away they hear a little girl's voice trying to join in.

Everyone falls silent.

Lily? Amy shouts. Lily, is that you?

Quiet. Only the sweet smell of damp leaves.

We believe in fairies, everyone chants again, but more cautiously. The triplets roll their drums. We believe in fairies.

And they hear the same little girl's voice trying to join in, now becoming louder and louder.

Until it is right above them.

They shine their flashlights up: Lily's head peeks out from the dense, fiery foliage erupting from the mid-high tentacles of a gigantic oak. Her face is stained a dark reddish-purple, and she is wearing a mistletoe crown.

iv

16

We've found Lily! We've found Lily! Shout Sam and Jude, scrambling with racing, elated hearts and the exciting expectation of glory through the forest toward the farm.

They bump into four police officers raking the ground for evidence.

We've found Lily! Sam and Jude repeat. We've found Lily!

Where? the police officers demand urgently, unhooking their walkie-talkies.

Up a tree! Sam replies.

The police officers are flabbergasted.

In the forest just back there, Jude adds. Amy and some other children are looking after her.

Alive and well? one of the police officers asks.

Yes! Jude and Sam effervesce.

Take us to her, another police officer orders.

Wait, says a third police officer. So all of you triplets are safe too?

Of course we're all safe, answers Sam, bewildered.

And who are these "other children"? the same officer quizzes.

They're all from the village, Jude explains. We walked down there ourselves, and then we met the minister, Jacob Jones, who made us all go back to his house in his car. But of course we ran away as soon as possible to try and find Lily.

The police officers exchange meaningful, businesslike looks.

These must be the other children who were seen getting into the car, one of them says. He turns to Sam and Jude. So all the children who got into Jacob Jones's car are here now?

Yes, they reply.

Where does this Jacob Jones live? the same police officer demands.

As soon as Jude has given them an answer, two of the police officers speak with deep, urgent voices into their walkie-talkies and head for Jacob Jones's vicarage.

The remaining two follow Jude and Sam to a thoroughly begrimed Lily, who has wrapped her feet in large leaves and is refusing to budge from her fairy tree palace, where she has a hoard of juicy plums.

☙

Beth opens the door in answer to a playful rat-tat-tat-tat. Police Officer Number One beams at her, a half-eaten king-size Mars Bounty bar in his hand.

We've found them all, he announces. Lily and the triplets, and they're all in good health. He takes a big bite from his Bounty bar. And our men are right now on their way to arrest the perpetrator.

Beth nearly collapses with relief. Thank God, she says, leaning her hand and pressing her weight down onto the windowsill of the porch. Thank God. She feels warmth rush over her as if she were Pygmalion's statue coming to life. Where did you find them?

⌒

When the young smiley couple, who want the organist to play the Wedding March from Mendelssohn's *A Midsummer Night's Dream* at the end of their service, eventually leave, Jacob Jones looks out the window to check on the children.

But of course they aren't there. He sees nothing except for his normal naked fields reaching out to the forest that bridges his land and Beth's. He panics. And of all the unpleasant emotions, Jacob Jones most detests panic. When the unfamiliar butts out the familiar; when the arrow shoots off from his narrow meter of expectation out to a chilly, dismal, alien region that he wishes to become acquainted with only through the television, from the comfort of his cozy sofa.

Drat! He hurries out of the room, catching his trousers on the sharp corner of the coffee table and tearing them, shakes off his slippers, and pulls on his Wellington boots. He opens the front door into the vibrant light of a midafternoon in late summer in the country.

❦

Beth races up the stairs, taking two at a time, and bumps into Joseph, whom she envelops in a huge hug, on the landing.

The triplets and Lily have been found alive and well! she tells him, all radiance. And it was the triplets themselves who found Lily—she was hiding up an oak tree!

So there was no Mushroom Man after all, concludes Joseph.

I'm not sure about that, says Beth, her face clouding over. The police are on their way to arrest someone now.

Thank goodness for that, says Joseph, feeling his tummy turn.

Beth releases him and runs down the corridor.

Does that mean I can leave the house and go to Nest's now? asks Joseph.

I suppose so! Beth answers, cheery again, before she bursts into Charlotte's bedroom.

Charlotte is lying on the bed with her eyes closed and her nose in the air, and Mr. Newman is slumped contritely on the floor beside her.

Lily has been found alive and well! exclaims Beth. The triplets spotted her hiding up an oak tree in the forest. Beth rushes over to a speechless Charlotte and plants a huge, firm kiss on her right cheek, which is already wet with the first tears of release. And the police are on their way right now to arrest the perpetrator.

Mr. Newman gets up on his knees, grabs Charlotte's left hand, brushes his lips over it, and brings it to his cheek. The cold ruby of her wedding ring on his warm skin makes him shiver.

Charlotte is finally able to collect herself. She flings off her bed-sheets like an insect shedding an old skin and jumps out of bed.

Beth opens her arms, ready to hug her sister. Charlotte instinctively runs into them and lets herself be hugged. A cathartic hug, a sunshine hug; Beth hugs like their mother—fully, tightly, and giving off the delicate smell of daffodils.

Beth is fighting back tears.

Mr. Newman stands beside his wife attentively, though ignored by her, as silent as her shadow, which is half on the floor and half still on the bed. And he realizes that, however often he may stray from her, he cannot ever leave her. He needs her. He is part of her. Together they have created a beautiful child called Lily.

Charlotte pulls away from Beth. Take me to my little darling, she says.

❦

It's not blood, it's plum juice, corrects Lily, as the police officer who has climbed the tree to rescue her stares in horror at her bespattered skin and clothes and the nest of mistletoe tangled in her luminous stream of hair.

The police officer is tongue-tied. After a moment he recovers. How on earth did you get up here?

In a unicorn-driven carriage, Lily answers simply.

Jesus Christ, the police officer mutters. He draws a reluctant Lily, who is crawling with fruit flies, carefully toward him and into his arms.

And it galloped up so fast that I nearly fell out and smacked my head open on the ground.

Jesus Christ, the police officer repeats, feeling dizzy as he slowly lowers Lily into the outstretched arms of another police officer at the foot of the tree.

The triplets rush over to Lily and smother her with kisses.

The other children stand back and watch and feel awkward, as if they have been dragged along by a friend to the birthday party of someone they don't know. The boy with the green spiky hair is anxiously awaiting an appropriate moment to ask for the Liquorice Spiders. Dick is thinking about the monkey bars. They all want to go home.

Lily, we were so worried about you, says Amy. We feared the Mushroom Man and the fairies would make you invisible forever.

Lily smiles.

In light of what has happened, I don't think it's appropriate to keep joking around about this fairy tale, scolds the police officer. He is cradling Lily and wrapping his jacket around her.

Jude turns and throws him a disgusted look. If it hadn't been for us, who took this fairy tale and Lily's words absolutely seriously, and convinced the fairies that we believed in them, she answers sharply, Lily would never have been found.

The two police officers sternly approach Jacob Jones, who is pacing his front fields in distress.

Are you Jacob Jones? they ask.

Yes.

The helicopter is now directly above them, confining them in a pool of shadow.

You are under arrest for the abduction of twelve children, one of them announces, pulling a pair of handcuffs out of his jacket pocket. Anything you say can be used against you.

Daddy's here! Lily says softly when she sees her parents and Beth running down the slope to meet them all.

Oh my God! shrieks Charlotte, when Lily's stained face and hands come into focus. She's covered in blood! She's covered in blood!

It's plum juice, corrects a police officer. There's no need to worry, she's entirely unhurt.

Oh my God, says Charlotte again, staring at Lily's mistletoe crown.

Beth kisses her niece on the forehead and shakes the two policemen's hands warmly before gathering her daughters around her and affectionately rubbing her face against the tops of their heads, the way a lioness might sniff and lick her cubs.

You silly, silly little pests, she murmurs.

Mr. Newman lets Charlotte hug Lily first. He stands and waits and smiles hard at their side.

Lily, my precious, precious princess, cries Charlotte. She lifts Lily, packaged in navy nylon like a special present, out of the police officer's arms and holds her tightly to her chest. She rocks her back and forth like a baby, not caring about her stench and stickiness and the fruit flies. Lily, my precious baby, don't ever run away like that again.

Lily doesn't respond. She smiles faintly at her father from her mother's shoulder before closing her eyes and falling asleep from weakness and exhaustion.

Joseph and Nest have decided to follow the stream that meanders through their farms to its mouth, where it gushes into the river. They paddle and splash through the icy mountain water sprinkled with the glitter of late-afternoon sun until they reach the mini-waterfall that is the stream's end.

They step up onto the bank and, arm in arm, watch the stream water spill never-endingly and unhesitatingly over the edge, a silky, elegant sheet to be united with its master.

And then eventually it will end up in the sea, says Nest.

I'm not following it as far as the sea.

Nest looks up at him with glistening, mischievous eyes. What a good idea!

It's miles and miles away, Nest. It would take days.

Oh, you do exaggerate, Josie.

Well, it is certainly a very, very long day's walk away.

Let's do it tomorrow, Nest begs. Let's. We'll get up early. We'll take a picnic with chocolate cupcakes. We'll pick blackberries and gooseberries on the way, and when we get to the sea . . .

She wraps both her arms around his neck.

Oh, Josie, think of smelling the salty sea!

Joseph smiles. He has never felt more in love with her. He pecks her on the tip of her nose. Whatever you want, he says.

⟨❀⟩

And where did these other children come from? asks Beth, registering the village pick-ups hovering at a distance.

From the village, Amy replies. She turns and signals for them to come forward. And if it hadn't been for them, she says proudly, when they are within earshot, the fairies probably wouldn't have been convinced enough to bring Lily back to us.

Beth looks troubled. So these are the children who also got into the man's car with you?

The triplets glance up, puzzled, at their mother.

Yes, replies Jude. Jacob Jones insisted on taking all of us back to his house.

Jacob Jones! Beth says loudly.

The policemen look across at her.

Beth takes her arms away from the triplets and stares down at them sternly. I want you to be absolutely truthful and tell me exactly what happened from the moment you left the house, she orders.

17

A terrible misunderstanding, Beth explains over the phone to Jacob Jones when the facts have been established and Jacob Jones released. I can't apologize enough. The line is fuzzy and crackling and crossed with a conversation between a man and a woman chatting animatedly in Spanish, merging two separate worlds.

It's no one's fault, least of all yours, Beth, Jacob Jones assures her. In any event, I should have rung you straightaway to tell you the triplets were with me. Instead I got caught up with this couple who came around . . .

You shouldn't have done anything differently, Jacob.

The line fuzzes and crackles even more disobediently. The crossed line goes silent for a moment, and then the male voice says tenderly, *Te amo, Esperanza.*

At least everyone's safe and well, thanks be to God, Jacob Jones garbles.

Thanks be to God, Beth repeats. Thanks be to God.

A pause.

May I pop around tomorrow to see how you all are? Jacob Jones asks cautiously.

Oh, please do, says Beth. Come for afternoon tea and you can meet my sister, niece, and brother-in-law.

I'm looking forward very much indeed. Take care.

Beth slowly slots the receiver back into place and looks out the window at her fields, now free of strangers, basking in the brilliant and ephemeral golden light of the magic hour. She wonders whether, in fact, Charlotte will stay until tomorrow, whether this is a new beginning or a foregone conclusion. And she wonders whether she could ever love Jacob Jones, for whom she has enormous affection as a friend and about whom she sometimes even coyly dreams, and doubts she could. She knows that, although her husband is dead, the love they had for each other lives and shines unsuppressed and unsurpassable in their beautiful children. Their beautiful children, who remind her every day of what is wondrous, but what is shut off in the past for her now, what can never be brought back.

⋅✍○

Charlotte and Mr. Newman are sitting stiffly next to each other on the flimsy plastic chairs in the waiting room of the children's ward of

Cardiff Hospital. Lily has just had an examination and is being treated for dehydration and mild hypothermia. Police Officer Number One and Police Officer Number Two are now questioning her, sitting on either side of the hospital bed that she is sharing with the cuddly toys the triplets have given her.

Charlotte and Mr. Newman hate hospitals. Hospitals remind Charlotte of the anxious hours spent in the IVF clinic, of the probability of her being infertile. Hospitals remind Mr. Newman of the unsympathetic, unrelenting disinfectant smell of the IVF clinic, of Charlotte's being inconsolably sad.

But this hospital waiting room in the children's ward is a lot more cheerful than a normal hospital waiting room. This hospital waiting room could almost not be in a hospital. There are colorful children's drawings on the wall, with bright, spiderlike suns that take up half the picture, and faces with enormous smiles that nearly touch the eyes. There are toys and games to jolly along the time here. There is even a television-and-video set playing cartoons.

And most of the children waiting with their parents here are happy. They might be sick, but they are happy. Building a multicolored Lego skyscraper or dressing a Barbie or watching Pokémon makes them temporarily happy.

Charlotte and Mr. Newman sit in this room, surrounded by sick but happy children, waiting to see their own child.

Lily needs toys like these, Charlotte says. Children like these toys.

Mr. Newman nods. Definitely, he replies. He has always said that Lily needs these sorts of toys instead of books and books and piano lessons four times a week, but Charlotte has always disagreed. He wonders whether this is a gesture of reconciliation toward him on her part. He waits.

And I want Pavlova out of the house within the next two days, she tells him, quietly and firmly.

๑

So you were in the tree the whole time, Lily, sums up Police Officer Number One, looking exhausted.

I was in my fairy tree palace the whole time, Lily answers softly, her face gaunt and expressionless.

Right. Police Officer Number One wipes his forehead. And the Mushroom Man is your imaginary friend.

He's the friend of the fairies who turned me into an invisible fairy like him.

Right.

Could you tell us a bit about your Wellies, which we found not far from where you were, Police Officer Number Two asks gently. And the nine plum stones that were right by them.

They were the leftovers from the invisible-making process, Lily replies. The plum stones were left over from when the Mushroom Man was making me some magic fairy plum juice, and the Welly material was too tough to be made invisible with the rest of me. Anyway, it didn't matter: fairies don't wear Wellies, they wear dainty fairy leaf shoes.

Police Officer Number One and Police Officer Number Two look at each other.

And where were you the two previous times you went missing? inquires Police Officer Number One.

In the Mushroom Man's fairy tree palace, which is right next door to where my fairy tree palace is. And he lets me have all the things to eat I'm not allowed at home, he lets me watch all the fun shows on his giant television screen, and he takes everything I say seriously.

⌒

Just before nightfall, Beth drives down to the village with the triplets. She follows the police van that is returning the triplets' recruits to their homes, as she has told the triplets that they have to apologize to the parents of the children for causing them so much worry.

The police van stops first at Dick's home, a one-bedroom flat above a fish-and-chip shop.

His mother opens the door, holding her still-shrieking baby.

Dick! She hugs him with her free arm. She turns to the police officer, who has already explained everything over the phone. Thank you so much for bringing him safely home.

All in a day's work, ma'am, the police officer replies.

The triplets come into view from behind the corner. Dick's mother jumps.

We're so sorry to have caused you so much worry, Amy says earnestly. But I just want you to know that Lily might never have been found if it hadn't been for the additional conviction of your son Dick.

Both Dick's mother and the police officer look curiously and amusedly at the eleven-year-old girl with braids who is speaking so properly yet nonsensically.

That's quite all right, answers Dick's mother, not knowing what else to say.

Do you really think I will be able to get to the end of the monkey bars now? asks Dick.

I'm positive about it, says Amy, beaming at him.

She starts to go down the stairs, then turns back and winks at him.

✺

Mr. Newman steps into the telephone booth in the hospital corridor and picks up the receiver.

Pavlova is in Kensington Gardens reading her *Vogue* magazine and chewing on a piece of Hollywood gum, savoring her last English moments. Her cell phone rings. She picks it up.

It's me, Mr. Newman announces in a foreboding voice.

Has Lily been found?

She's fine. She was hiding up a tree.

Thank goodness. Pavlova feels relief ripple through her, warming the tips of her fingers and toes. If everything is back to normal now, maybe she should think twice about going home. . . .

Pavlova, Mr. Newman begins, Charlotte knows.

Pavlova freezes. How?

She refused to tell me, but that's beyond the point anyway.

Pavlova feels her tummy churn.

I'm so sorry, but I think you're going to have to leave.

I was already planning to leave, Pavlova spits back, shocked and hurt and hating.

We'll pay you off well.

We: The word rings in her ears. Good, she replies icily.

When can you leave?

I've already booked my flight, for tomorrow.

We might miss you, then.

What a shame.

I'll transfer money into your account over the Internet tonight.

Do.

I'm sorry it had to end like this.

Pavlova presses the off button and bursts into tears.

Mr. Newman replaces the receiver and stares at it for a moment before picking it up again.

Can you give me the number for Tiffany's on Bond Street in London, please. . . .

The police van makes its last stop at the house of the boy with the green spiky hair. It is one of the nicest houses in the village, perched on top of the hill, with a glorious view of the valley, red geraniums frothing out neatly from stylish window boxes.

The boy's mother opens the door. She is plastered in striking makeup.

Oscar! She plants a firm burgundy-lipstick kiss on his cheek.

Oscar winces, clutching his bag of Liquorice Spiders.

The triplets apologize. Oscar's mother doesn't listen—she just laughs and kisses them on the cheek, and the police officer too.

They turn to leave, and Oscar follows, even though his mother tries to stop him.

I like being out alone at night, he tells the triplets. I like talking to the drunks outside the pub after closing time and getting them to buy me cigarettes and doing all the other things I know my mum would disapprove of.

18

You can go in and see her now, says a plump, smiley nurse wearing a Mickey Mouse hat with huge ears.

Charlotte and Mr. Newman jump up from their chairs and follow the nurse down a bright yellow corridor and around a corner, to where Police Officer Number One and Police Officer Number Two are standing outside Lily's room.

There are undoubtedly no suspicious circumstances, states Police Officer Number One flatly. He shakes Mr. Newman's hand, and then Charlotte's.

Are you absolutely sure? Charlotte asks anxiously.

One hundred percent.

But it's so odd for a young child to stay up in a tree for two days like that.

Police Officer Number One scratches his nose. That may be so,

Mrs. Newman, but it doesn't follow from that that there are suspicious circumstances involved.

Charlotte hesitates. I suppose not, she concedes in a soft voice.

There is not one shred of evidence to support the existence of a real-life Mushroom Man or the like, Police Officer Number One says. It was all in her imagination, Mrs. Newman. Her fertile little imagination.

꧂

Beth and the triplets are sitting around the kitchen table, munching a late dinner—fish and chips from the shop below Dick's flat.

If it hadn't been for us, Jude says, Lily might never have been found.

I must say, I can't get over the fact that the police officers didn't find Lily earlier, Beth says.

It's because she was invisible, Amy says for the tenth time that night.

Beth has learned that she only meets with angry rebuke if she says anything against this, so she remains silent.

It sounds ridiculous, but we're convinced that we're right, Amy continues. There are other worlds out there, Mum. Other worlds that we should be aware of, because they sometimes clash with our own.

Joseph and Nest enter the kitchen with crimson-splashed faces.

We followed the stream all the way to the river, Joseph laughs. And tomorrow Nest wants to follow the river to the sea.

Beth looks at Joseph and Nest, and in the untouchable twinkle in their eyes sees herself and her husband.

⊙≈

Charlotte rushes to her daughter's bedside and kisses her on both cheeks. How are you feeling, Lily, angel?

Mr. Newman tweaks Lily's foot, which is sticking out at the end of her bedcover.

Fine, thank you, replies Lily apathetically with a downcast face.

Have some nice pink marshmallows, Charlotte says. She opens the packet she brought for Lily and waves a marshmallow in front of her face.

Lily shakes her head. No, thank you.

"No, thank you" to a pink marshmallow!

Lily shakes her head again.

Good gosh! I'll have it, then. Charlotte pops it in her mouth.

Lily and Mr. Newman listen to Charlotte sucking and chewing away with labored enthusiasm.

Looking forward to starting school next week? Mr. Newman asks cheerfully.

Lily shakes her head once more. I want to stay up in my fairy tree palace forever and ever.

Charlotte looks at her daughter and feels her heart wrenching.

⊙≈

That night, Jacob Jones doesn't feel like writing poetry. And even if he felt like it, he would not be able to; he is too distracted. He suddenly sees his loneliness clinging to him like an invalid relation who insists on living with him and who has a lot of life in him yet.

Jacob Jones has loved many times, but not once has he satisfied his love. Such satisfaction has remained above and below him like Tantalus's grapes and water, which always appear so deliciously tempting, but which are always out of his reach.

It is a hugely sensitive matter for Jacob Jones, but before today, before the directness of Betty's friends at the funeral reception, before the horror of being momentarily taken for a child abductor, and before the bizarreness of hearing the confession of a Spanish lover, he could keep his feelings out of sight and untouchable under the carpet in the attic, in his poetry notebook with clouds on the front cover.

But no longer. These feelings have taken wing from his notebook and swarm around him like persistent mosquitoes determined to have a taste of his virgin blood. They won't go away, or even if they do, he is left with their big red bites like the marks from Cupid's arrows.

Beth has come to represent more than a romantic ideal. She has come to represent everything that his own life is lacking.

~ΘΟ

Pavlova is packing up all her belongings into one big brown suitcase. She is neatly folding her clothes and piling them in the suitcase, and fitting her bits and pieces—including the little glittery tins that contained the little almond biscuits Mr. Newman used to buy her—down the sides and into the corners.

She feels quietly content fitting all the belongings she has in the world into one rectangle she can then carry in one hand: everything of hers together in one place, not scattered about chaotically, everything of hers packed in a manner that will allow her to take herself off to anywhere in the world at any time.

But right now, Pavlova is looking forward to going back home. Back to friendly faces, back to familiar sights and sounds and smells, back to the warm, forgiving embrace of her mother, who will tell her that she is young and beautiful and has a rainbow of opportunities and that everything will be okay.

⚬

Charlotte sits at Lily's bedside, stroking her daughter's forehead. Mr. Newman has just left the room to look for a place where he can use the Internet.

Lily, darling, Charlotte whispers, with tears in her eyes. Lily, do you know how much your mummy and your daddy love you?

Lily is half asleep, but maybe there is acknowledgment in the faint twitch of the right corner of her mouth.

Lily, I know I've been a bit strict with you about not watching the television and about what toys you can have and things, but I was only doing what I thought best.

She watches Lily's face. It remains impassive.

But I realize now that perhaps I was wrong, Charlotte continues.

You can watch whatever fun shows you want, my darling, as soon as you've done your homework and piano practice. If there's a particular toy you want, Daddy and I will look into buying it for you.

Lily's eyelids flicker, and she opens her eyes: they stare, brilliant blue, into Charlotte's.

My fairy tree palace was better than all the fun shows and toys in the world put together, Lily murmurs. You can't imagine how magic it was, Mummy.

My darling, Charlotte says, sobbing, there is magic in other places.
Where?

Everywhere, darling, if you want to find it.

But you've never found it for yourself, Mummy, have you?

Charlotte is tongue-tied. Lily's eyes are locked in a fixed gaze with hers, gorgeous, indestructible sapphire.

Of course I have, she finally replies, mourning and marveling at the unnerving perceptiveness of her daughter. Especially when I was younger.

⌀

The triplets are tucked up, exhausted, under their fresh bedsheets. Princess Fairymostbeautiful's smile is larger than it was yesterday, and her diamond eyes are unclouded and glittering.

I wish there was more magic in the world, says Amy. I wish I could magic Felipe Llewellyn in love with me.

I wish I could magic myself a Filipino pirate, says Sam. With a beautiful wooden pirate ship with mottoes in Chinese carved on it.

I wish—begins Jude, searching the darkness of the room for the end of her sentence. I wish that Auntie Charlotte would stop hating Mummy. I wish that they become friends and that Mummy is happier.

❦

Beth is lying in the bathtub with half a cup of her favorite strawberry sundae bubble bath mixed into the warm water, listening to country-western music on the radio.

She has her eyes closed and lets her aches and anxieties dissolve into the soothing, sweet-smelling water. She thinks about how she and Charlotte used to take baths together when they were younger; about how they used to put extra bubble bath in when their mother wasn't looking, and tried to hide under the copious suds mountains; about how Charlotte used to reach out with her hand and, giggling, press her nipples in curiosity.

Beth steps out of the bath and rubs herself dry with a towel. She feels fresh and invigorated, and her skin is soft and smells nice. She says to herself, I will tell Charlotte I love her, and we will become friends again. Whatever it takes, even if it means biting my tongue and apologizing for things unnecessarily, we will become friends, sisters by nature as well as by name.

❦

Joseph and Nest are lying curled up together, asleep, like two twins in a womb. Joseph is dreaming of a place by the sea, an undiscovered cove that is the home of the most exotic fishes and sea plants and peachy-pink coral and where the water is a spectrum of blues and greens and the sand is a magic golden dust. Nest is dreaming of a place by the sea, an undiscovered stretch of beach where coconuts fall from the trees to the ground and split into perfect halves, and ever-ripe mangoes and papayas nearly burst with their sugary juices.

And they both dream of taking a boat to sea, like the Owl and the Pussy-Cat.

19

The telephone rings at nine the next, rainy morning.

Hello.

Beth, it's Charlotte.

Lottie! How's Lily doing?

She's fine, they're letting her out of hospital later this morning.

That's wonderful!

Charlotte can't help letting out a little laugh. Yes, it is wonderful. I'm so happy.

So I'm ringing to make sure that someone will be at home when we come back to pack up our stuff before returning to London tonight. We should be at the farm around twelve-thirty.

Of course I'll be in, but do you have to rush off so soon? Beth is desperately disappointed. Why don't you stay at least another night?

I think it's best if we get out of here as soon as possible, Charlotte replies pragmatically. In any event, Richard's got to get back for work, and I need to prepare Lily for school next week.

That's such a shame. I wanted to make up for the terrible time you've had here. I wanted . . . Beth hesitates.

Charlotte waits.

Never mind, sighs Beth.

But we should both spend this Christmas together with the children at Mum and Dad's, says Charlotte cheerfully. They would love to have us, I'm sure.

They'd be over the moon, replies Beth, not quite believing what she has just heard.

Great. So I'll see you around half-twelve.

I'll prepare some lunch, something quick.

That's kind of you.

I look forward to seeing you later, then.

Me too.

Charlotte hangs up.

Beth slowly puts the receiver into place and claps her hands together. With a bounce in her step, she walks from the studio to the kitchen to start chopping vegetables.

⌒

The doorbell rings. Pavlova, who is just about to leave and is gathering her last things, ignores it.

The doorbell rings again, for longer.

Pavlova curses, skids down the corridor in her socks, and opens the door.

A handsome young man in dark blue mailman's uniform, with slick black hair tied in a ponytail, stands staring at her.

A special delivery for Pavlova Mets, he announces.

That's me, she says, surprised. She signs the certificate of receipt, takes the package, and stares disbelievingly at the sender's address. Tiffany's. Thanks.

Have a good day.

Pavlova closes the door and opens the package. Inside is a small velvet box, and inside the small velvet box is the pair of sparkling diamond stud earrings she has always wanted. There is also a little card in the package, with the words "Apologies, Richard."

⟊

Joseph and Nest wake up with the cloudy dawn at five o'clock and are already nearly halfway to the Carmarthenshire coast. They follow the river snaking and shimmering through the wet rural landscape as if it were a normal road, looking out for silver flashes of trout shooting past instead of cars.

They pass big tail-tossing, grass-chomping cows that nonchalantly half raise their heads, flutter their long eyelashes, have a good crap, then drop their heads back down to the grass. They pass two old fishermen sitting under umbrellas, who touch the front tips of their caps in greeting and offer them a can of lager when they tell them they are following the river to the sea.

Bless you younguns, one of the fishermen says, handing them each a can. I remember when me and my missus tried to do the same thing when we were teenagers, but found too many diversions on the way to make it in one day. . . .

But it's possible, the other man says. If you continue at the pace you're going, you should be there by evening.

Joseph and Nest thank them and hurry on their way.

⤚◯

Beth is cooking and the triplets are cleaning. The house smells of lemon cleaning spray and spaghetti bolognaise and expectation, and the record player is spinning out Spanish dances.

Beth is chopping. Juicy tomatoes, fat cucumbers, crunchy iceberg lettuce. Chop chop chop. Into circles and squares and strips. Chop chop chop. Electric-yellow peppers, sweet home-grown carrots, fleshy mushrooms. Chop chop chop. Under the knife, off the chopping board, into the salad bowl.

Sam is hoovering the stairs, Jude is sweeping the corridor, and Amy is polishing the banister. They whirl and wiggle to the beat, and wolf whistle at the end of each track.

When they have finished, they change into clean clothes, secretly take a spray from the bottle of lavender eau de cologne, which they have noticed in front of their mother's moisturizing cream by the sink in the bathroom since this morning, and go downstairs to the living room, where they perch on the windowsill and look out for Mr. Newman's car.

❦

Beth and the triplets open the front door into the rain to see Mr. Newman walking through the front gate with Lily on his shoulders and Charlotte following under an umbrella.

The three girls run out and reach their hands up to Lily. Mr. Newman lowers her from his shoulders and lets them carry her through the doorway on a throne they construct by crossing their arms one over another.

Beth strokes Lily's head as she is ceremoniously brought into the house, and kisses Mr. Newman on the cheek and squeezes his hand as he enters. Then she raises her arms to embrace her sister. Charlotte pulls down her umbrella, shakes off the rain, puts the umbrella to the side, and raises her own arms. They draw each other close. For a moment they are one: clothes, hair, skin touching; warmth and smell mingling. Beth wants to cry. Charlotte wants to cry.

But they just stare into each other's eyes, eyes that are a soft green, like their mother's, and that tell a stranger Beth and Charlotte are sisters, and they smile at each other.

Lunch is ready whenever you want it, says Beth.

❦

Pavlova decides she doesn't want the diamond earrings. They are gorgeous and she has always wanted them, but they represent everything about *him* and their base relationship. Taking them home with her would be like preserving one of her greatest mistakes.

So she decides to leave them to Lily. To Lily they will be just a pretty pair of earrings to wear when she is older, Pavlova thinks. Lily will like them, and they will be a nice surprise for her to come home to after all that has happened.

Pavlova leaves the Tiffany's box on Lily's bedside table with a folded piece of paper on which she has written: "Dear Lily, take care. I enjoyed every minute of looking after you. With love from P, xxxxxxxxxxx."

⌀

It's like Christmas! Jude exclaims, as she walks into the kitchen, seeing the red-and-green paper chains her mother has hung across the ceiling, and the Christmas crackers placed neatly next to the knives.

I thought Lily would like it, Beth says, taking out the plates warming in the stove.

I'm sure she will. Charlotte helps Beth lay the plates on the table.

Mr. Newman stands in a corner and looks at the delicately joined red and green circles. Exquisite, he says. The paper chains are absolutely exquisite, Beth, I must say.

The girls made them last Christmas, Beth replies. They made so much of an effort with them that I kept them.

Amy and Sam come into the kitchen with Lily, having helped her to wash her hands for lunch. Lily looks at the decorations and smiles.

It's just like the dining room in my fairy tree palace, she murmurs, as Amy helps her onto a chair with two cushions.

Beth and Mr. Newman watch Charlotte's face fall. Beth turns to drain the spaghetti and asks Mr. Newman to open the bottle of Chianti in the cupboard.

It won't hurt to drive after just one glass, Beth says.

⟰

Joseph and Nest are tipsy. Their hair, faces, necks, and hands, the parts peeping out of their hoodless mackintoshes, are wet and glistening and salty, and they keep falling about in fits of hysterics about nothing in particular.

We need the Mushroom Man, jokes Nest.

What?

We need some frickin' umbrellas.

We've got the beer instead, says Joseph. That's good enough to keep me going.

The Beer Men . . . , Nest muses.

What?

The Beer Men are our Mushroom Man, the friends of Joseph and Nest.

⟰

Lunch is sad because Lily is sad. Lily's mood puts a damper on everyone and everything. She sits at the head of the table, propped up on her cushions, playing with, instead of eating, her spaghetti bolognaise. Her eyes are lifeless and her expression vacant. She is silent.

Lunch is soured: the basil flavor of the bolognaise, the sweetness of the salad, the velvetiness of the wine, the newfound spirit of sisterly respect and reconciliation. Mr. Newman makes bad jokes that no one gets and everyone laughs forcedly at. Sam spills her glass of Coca-Cola. Amy is afflicted by unsuppressible hiccups. Beth mentions Pavlova and asks how much longer she will be staying in England.

Not much longer, I hope, Charlotte says curtly.

I think she's leaving today actually, Mr. Newman replies breezily.

Beth watches them both closely, remembers Lily's previous mention of Pavlova, and understands. And this confirms the distrust Beth has felt toward Mr. Newman from the moment she first met him with her husband at her parents' house in London: Mr. Newman told her that he went to a grammar school, and her husband that he went to Gordonstoun.

Beth is dreadfully pained for her sister's sake, and she cannot look Mr. Newman in the eye for the rest of lunch.

*

Pavlova takes one last look at the house as she rides off in the taxi for Heathrow Airport.

She is glad that she can leave it all behind her in that house, that house which will never get up and follow her, that house which looks the same as it did when she first arrived.

That house with window eyes, which she has left with all the curtain eyelids wide open.

20

Mr. Newman has put their luggage in the cars, and they are ready to go. Everyone except Lily gathers in the hallway to say good-bye, and everyone is uneasy because she is throwing a tantrum and refusing to budge from the top of the stairs.

I don't want to go home! she wails. I want to go back to my fairy tree palace.

The triplets try to console her by offering her their gold-glitter drums.

We used them to communicate with the fairies, Amy explains, so you might find them useful too.

Charlotte and Beth look distressed. Mr. Newman clears his throat and glances impatiently at his Rolex, which is back on his wrist.

Lily quiets for a moment and sniffles. Thank you, she mumbles. And then she starts crying again.

Come on, now, says Mr. Newman firmly, climbing the stairs and scooping her up. We have to get going.

Lily screams. No! she shouts. I don't want to go back home.

We all have to do things we don't want to at times, replies Mr. Newman.

Lily is bawling.

Charlotte strokes her forehead. Come on, now, darling, say good-bye to Beth and Amy and Sam and Jude.

Lily quiets again. Put me down, she demands of her father.

Mr. Newman puts her down.

Lily goes to Beth and her cousins and gives each of them a hug and a peck on the cheek.

When Lily hugs her, Amy picks her up and swings her around. I want children just like you, she tells Lily.

Lily smiles. Everyone laughs.

◆

The clouds are clearing, and Joseph and Nest can make out the sea in the distance—a frothing turquoise strip kneaded by the wind and disappearing into the horizon.

Nest jumps up and down, and then, stretching her arms out, spins around and around until she falls to the ground from dizziness.

Joseph jumps on top of her and tickles her until she is screaming for him to stop.

And then he kisses her salty lips.

❧

Lily is strapped in the back of Charlotte's car, looking miserable, despite the fact that her cousins are making funny faces at her through the window. Her mistletoe crown, which she has vigorously insisted should not be discarded, lies withered on her lap.

Mr. Newman kisses Beth on both cheeks, shakes his nieces' hands, waves at Lily, and walks to his car.

Charlotte takes Beth's hands and squeezes them gently, and then they hug: tightly, warmly, like sisters who understand each other. Beth can feel Charlotte's heart beating fast. The triplets watch, and then smile at one another.

I'll ring in a few days to see how you are, Charlotte says.

That would be wonderful.

Charlotte approaches the triplets and kisses them all on the cheek before getting into her car. And love to Joseph and Nest, she calls, leaning out the window before starting the engine.

❧

Joseph and Nest can hear the rumble and roar of the sea as it thunders onto the long exposed stretch of sand, and they smell its sharp fishiness and saltiness. The river is wide and fast and furious now, fearlessly heading toward its end.

They are running.

They are running toward the blue and the sound and the smell.

⊰⟳

Charlotte is gone, but Beth has never felt so close to her. Charlotte and Lily have gone, but their presence is everywhere—in the smells they have left behind, in their blond hairs on the pillows they used, in the fresh lilies of the valley that Charlotte sneaked into the vase in the bedroom when she returned from Cardiff, which now ring out their whiteness.

And Lily has created a new magic. A magic breathed onto everyone as imperceptibly as the whisper of an invisible fairy.

⊰⟳

Lily is the first to see the rainbow.

Mummy, look! she squeaks ecstatically. Look at the rainbow!

Charlotte sees the rainbow and stares at it in awe: mighty, majestic, acrobatically spanning the sky with wonder. It's beautiful, she says.

It's Princess Fairymostbeautiful's upside-down smile! Lily screams. Hello, Princess Fairymostbeautiful!

A smile, restrained at first, but then liberated, tickles and ripples across Charlotte's lips.

⊰⟳

Jacob Jones is the next to see the rainbow: he rings Beth's doorbell and, looking at the sky, catches sight of the fabulous stream of colors injected into the sky in the shape of a threshold. A gigantic and gorgeous threshold. A divine threshold.

Beth opens the door. Hi! she says cheerfully.

Come and look at the rainbow, says Jacob, touching her back with his right hand and guiding her outside.

Beth marvels. She touches Jacob's back too. Lightly. But her hand feeds sharp warmth into every bone in his body.

Jacob stares at Beth's eyes which are laughing and looking at the rainbow. You're incredible, Beth, he can't help saying.

Beth flashes her eyes at him and blushes. She giggles, looks back at the rainbow, and then turns to face him properly. She kisses him quickly and softly on the lips.

☙

Mr. Newman stares at the rainbow dominating the sky in all its splendor and sees it as the signature of a new beginning. He glances in the rearview mirror at Charlotte's car following and catches sight of her smiling face and Lily's hand waving out the window.

He picks up his cell phone and calls Charlotte's number.

Hello.

I love you, Charlotte, he says. I love you and our Lily so much.

There is a long pause.

I'm sorry beyond anything I can even begin to describe.

There is an even longer pause.

I want to make us work again, darling Lottie. His voice is desperate, almost childlike. I want to make us be happy together—for Lily's sake, if nothing else—more than anything else in the world.

Charlotte wrinkles her forehead and swallows hard to fight back surging tears.

We can try, she replies quietly.

They both drive toward the painted bridge of a thousand colors.

⁊◯

The triplets rush out the front door to admire the rainbow. They are so excited that they do not notice Jacob Jones and their mother, who are now shuffled up close together on the bench in the garden.

That is magic, declares Amy, gazing at the glorious mountain drawn in the sky. I wish I could save some of it up in a jam jar.

I wonder what it tastes like, muses Sam.

Maybe it's Daddy saying hello, says Jude.

⁊◯

The rainbow has melted, the sun is setting, and Joseph and Nest have reached their destination. They kick their Wellingtons onto the sand, rip off their socks, roll their trousers to their knees, and head for the breakers frothing forward to meet them, glistening with the last sparkles of sunlight.

They jump and chase and flee the icy waves, which nibble farther and farther into the shore, and they watch the falling of a brilliantly clear blanket of stars.

—

And hand in hand, on the edge of the sand,

> *They danced by the light of the moon,*
> *The moon,*
> *The moon,*
> *They danced by the light of the moon.*

◈

Lily enters her room and sees the Tiffany's box on her bedside table. She opens it and gasps at the diamond studs gleaming at her from their velvet bed.

Princess Fairymostbeautiful's eyes! Lily is elated.

She reads the folded note. And she has even written a nice message for me, Lily thinks.

Lily puts the box and the note under her pillow and promises herself that she will bury them at the bottom of the garden for safekeeping in the morning.

◈

Look! Sam shouts from up in the tree Lily hid in. Lily's present to the Mushroom Man is here, with her thank-you card.

She must have forgotten to give them to him, concludes Jude.

Leave them there, says Amy. Leave them there for Daddy.